Barbara Cartland, the
who is also an historian,
television personality,
over 390 million over the

She has also had many historical works published and has written four autobiographies as well as the biographies of her mother and that of her brother, Ronald Cartland, who was the first Member of Parliament to be killed in the last war. This book has a preface by Sir Winston Churchill and has just been republished with an introduction by Sir Arthur Bryant.

Love at the Helm, a novel written with the help and inspiration of the late Earl Mountbatten of Burma, Uncle of His Royal Highness the Duke of Edinburgh, is being sold for the Mountbatten Memorial Trust.

Miss Cartland in 1978 sang *An Album of Love Songs* with the Royal Philharmonic Orchestra.

In 1976 by writing 21 books, she broke the world record and has continued for the following 7 years with 24, 20, 23, 24, 24, 25 and 22. In the Guinness Book of Records she is listed as the world's top-selling author.

In private life Barbara Cartland, who is a Dame of Grace of the Order of St John of Jerusalem, Chairman of the St John Council in Hertfordshire and Deputy President of the St John Ambulance Brigade, has fought for better conditions and salaries for Midwives and Nurses.

She has championed the cause for old people, had the law altered regarding gypsies and founded the first Romany Gypsy camp in the world.

Barbara Cartland is deeply interested in Vitamin therapy, and is President of the National Association for Health.

Her designs 'Decorating with Love' are being sold all over the USA and the National Home Fashions League made her, in 1981, 'Woman of Achievement'.

Barbara Cartland's book *Getting Older, Growing Younger*, and her cookery book *The Romance of Food* have been published in Great Britain, the USA, and in other parts of the world.

She has also written a children's pop-up book entitled *Princess to the Rescue*.

BARBARA CARTLAND

THE SECRET OF
THE MOSQUE

A Pan Original
Pan Books London and Sydney

First published 1986 by Pan Books Ltd
Cavaye Place, London SW10 9PG
9 8 7 6 5 4 3 2 1
© Cartland Promotions 1986
ISBN 0 330 29168 8
Printed and bound in Great Britain by
Hunt Barnard Printing Ltd, Aylesbury, Bucks

Barbara Cartland's Experience on Health

1930-2
Studied herbal medicine with the famous Mrs Leyll of Culpepper.

1931-3
A patient and a student of Dr Dengker of Baden-Baden. First use of olive oil as an internal treatment of liver complaints, colitis and inflammation of the bowel.

1930-7
Helped Lady Rhys Williams giving vitamin B to treat habitual abortion and malnutrition in distressed areas.

Studied the first use of vitamin E with brood mares and later for barren women.

1935 onwards
Worked with Dr Pierre Lansel, MD, first practitioner in England to give injections of vitamins B and C. Followed his experiments with hormones for rejuvenation and the Nieheims treatment of cell therapy. Studied with two eminent doctors the effect of oil injection on external haemorrhoids.

Studied the nutritional condition in her brother's Parliamentary Constituency, King's Norton Division of Birmingham, where there was malnutrition owing to low wages and unemployment.

Practised Yoga exercises and breathing with the only white Yogi in the world. Wrote in a monthly magazine on the subject.

Studied nutrition in Montreal and did two lecture tours in lower Canada during which visited a large number of schools and hospitals.

1939-45
County Cadet Officer for the St John Ambulance Brigade, Bedfordshire. Arranged first aid and home nursing lectures and discussed nutrition with doctors from overseas. Only Honorary Member of the Officers' Mess (Doctors and Psychiatrists) of 101 Convalescent Home, the largest Rehabilitation Centre in Great Britain.

Looked after 10,000 RAF and the US Flying Fortresses until the American Red Cross arrived.

Studied nutrition of the troops and the conditions in the Prisoner of War camps.

As Lady County Welfare Officer of Bedfordshire Voluntary Junior Commander (Captain) ATS, dealt with innumerable complaints about food from RAF camps, Secret Stations and Searchlight Posts and with the health and employment of pregnant mothers from all three Services. Studied conditions in the hospitals treating the women in the armed Services.

1945
Was introduced in America to the first B-Complex Multi-Vitamin (synthetic) capsule. On return home was closely in touch with the American manufacturers of vitamins, receiving regular reports, literature and supplies until the Organic Vitamin Company opened at Hemel Hempstead.

1950
Vitamins saved her life. Kept fifty-two farrowing sows on her farm in Hertfordshire and experimented by giving them

and the boars brewers yeast from a brewery. For four years they held the record production for Great Britain with an average of eleven a litter. Method copied by Sir Harry Haig for Ovaltine. Her prize-winning bull was given vitamin E injections.

1955
Published: *Marriage for Moderns, Be Vivid Be Vital, Love, Life and Sex, Vitamins for Vitality*, etc.
Began her lectures on health.

Became a County Councillor of Hertfordshire, on Education and Health Committees for nine years.

Studied nutrition with regard to school meals. Deeply concerned with the health and conditions of old people. Was so horrified at the way they were fed in some homes, and their general treatment, that her daughter, then Viscountess Lewisham, visited 250 homes all over Great Britain.

Following her reports and Barbara Cartland's and the tremendous press publicity involved, the Minister for Housing and Local Government (The Rt. Hon. Duncan Sandys. M.P.) instigated an enquiry into the 'Housing and Conditions of the Elderly'.

Was on the Managerial Committee of several old people's homes and a Patron of Cell Barnes, the largest home for retarded children in Great Britain.

Visited and inspected innumerable hospitals, clinics and homes for the elderly and for children. Started her fight for better salaries and conditions for Midwives and Nurses, which brought her into close contact with many of the teaching hospitals and Royal College of Midwives.

1958
Was host to Professor Ana Aslan, founder of H3, on her first visit to England at the invitation of 400 doctors. Also tried acupuncture and the Cryiac Method of holding a slipped rib or disc.

1960
Started to write monthly for *Here's Health*.

Co-founder of the National Association for Health.

Answered 5,000 letters a year – 10,000 in 1984. *The Magic of Honey* (1 million copies), doubled the sale of honey in Great Britain and over the world.

Lectured on health to:

The Southgate Technical College
The Queen Elizabeth College of Nutrition
The Polytechnic
The Hertfordshire Police Cadets
Two lectures in the Birmingham Town Hall to audiences of 2,500
Frequent lectures to Midwives, Universities, Rotary Clubs, etc.

1964-1978
Given a Civic Reception by the Mayor of Vienna for her work in the Health Movement.

Had private discussions on health, herbs and health foods with:

The Ministers of Health and Sciences in Mexico, Japan and India. Professors and scientists in Mysore working on the development of agriculture in the famine areas near Kerala with the India Ladies Committee and officials on health in Bombay, New Delhi and Mysore.

In touch with the Indian Guild of Service working among orphans, and in the poor areas in India, and saw the conditions among the first three million Pakistanis who moved into Calcutta in 1958.

Visited the new refugee areas in Hong Kong, was the first woman to visit (with the police) the Chinese border, seeing the conditions of the workers.

Visited Nepal and saw the insanitary conditions in Katmandu and the rat-infested refuse in the streets. Discussed the conditions with officials.

Visited hospitals, clinics and old people's homes in many parts of India, Bangkok, Hong Kong, Singapore, Switzerland, Austria and France.

Taken on a special visit with five doctors and scientists to inspect the Vitel Clinic in France.

Visited the slums of Delhi, Calcutta, Bombay, Phnom-Penh (Cambodia), Taiwan, Singapore, Rio, Harlem (New York), Glasgow, London, and had talks with the leading doctor in Istanbul and shown clinical trials undertaken.

Is closely in touch with the pioneers of the Health Movement in South Africa.

Invited – as a guest – to Yugoslavia, Germany and France.

1978
Visited Leningrad and Moscow and had talks with the scientists on old age problems and the use of Ginseng.

1984

A Dame of Grace of St John of Jerusalem; Chairman of the
St John Council, and Deputy President of the St John
Ambulance Brigade in Hertfordshire. One of the first
women in 1,000 years to be on the Chapter General; Presi-
dent of the Hertfordshire Branch of the Royal College of
Midwives; President of the National Association for
Health.

Author's Note

In 1880 the British recognised Abdurrahman Khan as Amir
of Kabul and undertook to require the admission of a
British Resident anywhere in Afghanistan.

As the British were preparing to leave, another British
force was annihilated near Kandahar by Ayub Khan.

Lord Roberts with 10,000 picked men started for Kandahar and on August 31st 1880 attacked and defeated Ayub
Khan.

The British then evacuated Afghanistan but when they
were gone Ayub Khan once more seized Kandahar only to
be defeated by the Amir – Abdurrahman. He then fled to
Persia.

The successors of the Young Ottomans were the young
Turks who finally in 1908 after an armed rising caused
Sultan Abdul Hamid to restore the Constitution.

Chapter One
1895

"I am afraid, Mama," Rozella said, "we shall have to sell the house!"

Her mother gave a cry of horror.

"Oh, no, darling, we cannot do that!"

"There is nothing else we can do, Mama. I have been thinking and thinking, and these bills keep growing larger every day."

Mrs Beverly sat down in a chair by the fireplace, clasping her hands together as if she felt she must control herself in front of her daughter.

"If we do . . have to . . leave," she said after a moment, "where could we . . go?"

Rozella sitting at the table with a pile of accounts in front of her made a hopeless gesture with her hands.

"I have no idea, Mama."

"But your father, we should not move him."

"How is he?" Rozella asked quickly. "And what did the Doctor say?"

"He said," Mrs Beverly replied slowly as if she were choosing her words, "that your father's heart is almost back to normal, but he will have to take great care of himself and of course have the . . right food to eat."

She looked at her daughter helplessly as she spoke and Rozella replied:

"That is what I expected. But Mama, how can we do it? I know the only thing we can do is to sell this house."

Mrs Beverly, who was still a very lovely woman, looked around the small sitting-room with an expression of despair on her face.

"We have been so happy here," she said as if she spoke to herself. "We came here after I had run away with your father, and the house always seemed to be full of sunshine."

"I love it too, Mama," Rozella said gently, "and I know it would hurt you dreadfully to move, but I feel it is the only thing we can do unless we are all to starve!"

Mrs Beverly gave a little cry of protest.

"That is one thing your father must not do! The Doctor was insistent that he should have plenty of chickens, milk and anything that would tempt him to eat. You know how fastidious your father is."

"He has been spoilt by his experience in travelling all over the world," Rozella said with a smile, "especially in France and even more so in the Middle East."

"Nanny has tried, we all have," Mrs Beverly said, "to make what he likes."

There was a little pause before Rozella said, and she felt she was being brutal:

"With what?"

There was silence, but the room seemed to vibrate with questions that could not be answered.

There was a distant knock on the front door and Rozella got up from the table.

"I will answer it," she said, "I know Nanny's doing your bedroom and will not hear it."

Nanny was the only servant they could afford. She had been with them since Rozella was born and never worried if her wages, which were very small anyway, were forgotten for months on end.

Because she had loved Rozella ever since she came into the world, she had become one of the family.

As Rozella walked towards the front door she thought that Nanny would mind leaving the little Manor house no less than her mother.

It seemed impossible that they should have to do so after

12

she had lived there all her life, but she had a feeling that because it was so attractive it should fetch quite a large price. That would enable them to take a small cottage, and for a time at any rate, to buy the food that was so necessary for her father.

She opened the front door and to her surprise she saw Ted Cobb, the postman outside.

"Hello, Ted!" she exclaimed, "why have you come back again?"

"Ye may well ask, Miss Rozella," Ted Cobb replied, in his broad Sussex accent. "Fer the second time this mornin' Oi've tramped down your drive an' me rheumatism's been real bad for the last few days."

"I am so sorry, Ted," Rozella said. "What is it this time?"

The postman took a long envelope from his bag which had an unusual amount of stamps on it.

"Special Delivery, Miss. A new idea from London, and not one that Oi likes whatever anyone else may feel about it!"

"I wonder what it can be," Rozella said. "I only hope it is not another bill."

"Whoever sent it spent enough money postin' it to ye," Ted smiled. "Well, Oi must be gettin' back an' Oi hopes Oi don't have to bring ye anythin' else till tomorrow mornin'."

"Thank you very much, Ted," Rozella said.

As she spoke she shut the front door, staring at the letter which she saw was addressed to her father in a strong, upright hand.

She thought as she took it back to the sitting-room that she must save the stamps for Farmer Jackson's little boy who was collecting them.

"What is it, darling?" her mother asked as she re-entered the sitting-room.

"A rather important looking letter for Papa," Rozella

13

replied. "It comes from London so I am sure it is not another bill."

"We must not worry your father with it," Mrs Beverly said quickly. "At least not until we know what it contains."

"Shall I open it, Mama?"

"Yes, you open it," Mrs Beverly said, "and I will just sit praying that by a miracle it is good news."

It flashed through both their minds that perhaps the Professor's publishers had sent them a royalty on one of his books.

Rozella knew this was very unlikely.

Her father's books, which were rather heavy treatises on different nationalities and their languages, although respected and admired by Scholars, were of no interest whatsoever to the general public.

When she thought about it, she remembered that the few pounds that they had received for last year's sales had come in three months ago.

She slit the envelope open neatly and drew out the contents.

It was a letter written on two pages of heavy, expensive writing-paper and mounted with a crest engraved over an address which she did not recognise.

She knew her mother was waiting and read in her soft, well-modulated voice:

Dear Beverly,

As soon as you receive this I wish you to proceed immediately to Dover and take the train overland to Constantinople where I will be waiting for you. I am leaving today on a very important mission and it is absolutely essential that you should be with me to help me as you have done before with the language of the very strange people we shall be meeting.

I expect you are aware of the many tensions in the

*Muslim world and the danger of revolutionary move-
ments inside the Ottoman Empire.*

*The Foreign Secretary is also deeply concerned by wild
rumours of crises within the British Empire which are
circulating around Europe. One is that the Suez Canal
has been seized by the Turks and leased to the Russians,
while the Mullah claims that the Faithful can never be hurt
by British bullets.*

*All this needs refuting, but the Foreign Secretary needs
more information than has reached him from Diplomatic
sources, and you and I know how that can best be obtained.*

*I shall look forward to seeing you in Constantinople as
soon as you can get there, and I enclose a first-class ticket
for the cross-channel steamer and for the train, or rather
trains, which will enable you to reach me as quickly as
possible.*

*I also enclose fifty pounds in bank-notes for your ex-
penses and a cheque for five hundred pounds as the first
half of your usual fee.*

*Kindly leave home as soon as you receive this, and if
there are any difficulties you can of course, contact my
secretary at the above address.*

*In these circumstances I expect you, and it is urgent, to
join me by the end of next week.*

Mervyn

Rozella was almost breathless by the time she finished
reading the letter and then as she looked at the enclosures
which it contained, she raised her head to say in an awe-
struck voice:

"Five hundred pounds, Mama!"

Mrs Beverly, who had listened attentively to what her
daughter had read, said:

"Lord Mervyn was always very generous, and when

Papa went on the last expedition with him – it must have been at least seven years ago – he paid him one thousand pounds."

Rozella put the cheque down on the table and smiled. Even to look at such a large sum made her feel excited.

Then she said wistfully:

"I suppose, Mama, it would not be possible for Papa to do this."

Mrs Beverly gave a cry of horror.

"No, of course not! It would kill him! The Doctor said he might easily have another heart attack, unless we were very careful."

She paused then added:

"You must send the letter back, with of course the cheque and the tickets, and explain how ill Papa is."

"But Lord Mervyn will already have left by now, Mama. He says so in the letter."

"Then I suppose that when he reaches Constantinople, his Secretary will be able to get in touch with him and tell him he must do whatever he has to do, alone."

"What does Lord Mervyn do?" Rozella asked. "I have heard Papa talking about him, but I suppose I was not really listening."

"Your father would not talk about it very much for the simple reason it was so secret. Then I do not know exactly what Lord Mervyn and Papa did together. Last time they went into Algeria and I believe it was a very dangerous mission, although your father did not tell me that until afterwards. It was very successful, however, and they obtained a great deal of information which the Foreign Office could not have had from any other source."

Rozella sat down opposite her mother and said incredulously:

"Are you telling me, Mama, that Papa was spying for the British Government?"

Mrs Beverly laughed.

16

"I suppose that was exactly what it amounted to! Lord Mervyn was sent to find out the truth of certain rumours which had been reported in England, and of course he needed Papa who could not only speak Arabic fluently, but also many of the different dialects in which he alone was proficient. He could communicate at first hand with all the different tribes and find out exactly what was happening."

"Then that is what he is asking Papa to do again," Rozella said reflectively.

Then lowering her chin a little she said:

"Lord Mervyn must be a very strange man to expect Papa to go at a moment's notice, however inconvenient it may be, just because he wants his help!"

"I am afraid that Lord Mervyn thinks there is no one more important than himself," Mrs Beverly said with a smile.

"Well, I think it is insulting!" Rozella said. "He has given orders to Papa, just as if he were one of his servants, to come here, do this, leave at once! How does he know if it is convenient for Papa to do such a thing?"

"Lord Mervyn believes that what he is concerned with takes precedence over everything else," Mrs Beverly said.

"Well, this time His Lordship is going to be disappointed!" Rozella said. "I wish I could see his face when he learns in Constantinople that there is going to be no one to help him. He will have to do everything by himself!"

"I am sure he will be very upset,' Mrs Beverly said. 'I believe he considered your father absolutely indispensable, but I shall never forget how worried and anxious I was during the last three months he was away, and I am so thankful he cannot go this time."

"I suppose, Mama," Rozella said slowly, "we could not keep the cheque he has sent Papa. It is everything we have prayed for."

"No, of course not!" Mrs Beverly said. "How could you think of such a thing!"

"I was only teasing," Rozella replied. "I will send it back, but it would have saved us from leaving the house and would provide Papa with delicious dishes and nourishing meals."

She rose to walk back to the table. Then as she stood looking down at the cheque for five hundred pounds signed with Lord Mervyn's strong, distinctive hand, she gave an exclamation.

"What is it?" her mother asked.

"I have just thought, Mama. Why should we send this cheque back when I can go instead of Papa? You know I can speak all the languages that Lord Mervyn requires almost as well as he can!"

"Once again you are teasing me," Mrs Beverly said. "Can you imagine what a commotion it would cause if you turned up instead of your father."

"I should be extremely useful," Rozella replied. "In his last book Papa wrote, there was quite a long passage in Turkish and he made me repeat every word that he used until I pronounced it perfectly. The same is true of any dialect that is spoken in Constantinople. I have been able to speak them all since I was in the nursery. Papa was certain of that."

Mrs Beverly knew this was true because her husband was one of the greatest experts in Turkish and Arabic and their many dialects.

It had amused him to make his only child, from her earliest possible age, speak to him not only in the classical manner that appertained to each country, but also in the dialects peculiar to the many different tribes in which he himself was a master.

"If you were a boy," Mrs Beverly said now, "it would be easy. In fact, because I am the one who sits at home I know how much you would enjoy the expedition, but unfortunately, darling, you are a girl, and a very attractive one."

Rozella sat down opposite her mother again.

"Let us think this out, Mama," she said. "Nothing is impossible in this world as we both know, and we are very aware that five hundred pounds has come into our hands as a direct answer to our prayers."

"What are you saying? What are you talking about?" Mrs Beverly asked.

"I am just thinking out how I could go in Papa's place, while you can stay here and spend five hundred pounds on getting him well."

"That is nonsense and you know it!" Mrs Beverly retorted. "How could you possibly travel alone to Constantinople, and after that anywhere with Lord Mervyn?"

"If Papa can do it, so can I," Rozella asserted.

"Looking like you do?" Mrs Beverly asked. "Do not be ridiculous! You are far too lovely, my darling, to travel anywhere alone, even from here to London."

"What you are saying," Rozella said slowly, "is that if I were middle-aged, plain and wore glasses, no one would bother me."

"You would still be a lady," Mrs Beverly said, "and ladies do not travel unattended."

"They can also lie unattended in a coffin from starvation," she retorted.

Mrs Beverly looked away from her daughter as if she was suddenly aware of how thin she was and how prominent the line of her chin and the bones of her wrists.

As if she was now genuinely afraid of what Rozella was thinking, she said:

"Very well, we will sell the house. I am sure we can find somewhere smaller where we can be quite comfortable."

"No, Mama!" Rozella said firmly. "We are not going to do that. We are going to be brave and, even if it is slightly unconventional, then you will have to tell yourself nothing is perfect in this very difficult world!"

"If you are talking about Constantinople," Mrs Beverly said quickly, "I will not have it! Do you understand,

19

Rozella? It is something you cannot possibly do!"

"Wait a minute, Mama. I have something to show you," Rozella said.

She rose to her feet and ran from the room, leaving her mother looking after her retreating figure with an expression of anxiety and perplexity.

Then when she was alone Mrs Beverly rose to go to the table and looked down as her daughter had, at the cheque for five hundred pounds.

She knew only too well what a difference it could make to their financial problems and the despair she had felt increasing, day by day, night by night.

Upstairs, lying listless in the bed they had shared ever since they were married with so much happiness, was her husband.

When she had run away with him she had only been eighteen.

As a young Oxford Don, the youngest in the whole University, he had come to her father's house to coach her brother.

Elizabeth had known from the moment she had met him that nothing in her comfortable, aristocratic home was more important than her love for Edward Beverly.

Apart from the fact that he was the best-looking man she had ever seen, he was much more than that.

It was a meeting of two people who were meant for each other since the beginning of time, and Edward Beverly believed they had already been together in a thousand previous incarnations only to be united in this one.

They were wildly happy, despite the fact that they were so very poor.

Edward Beverly had already made his mark in the academic world with his extraordinary knowledge of the languages of the Middle East.

He had also travelled a great deal and, at thirty-two, had been appointed to a Professorship at Oxford, while he was

20

already known to the Foreign Office for the information he had brought back to them from his travels.

He had a small income from his father and not much later he inherited the capital. It was not a great deal and the needs of his family resulted in his over-spending year by year.

It did not worry him particularly except that he longed to give his wife everything she wanted in the world, while the only thing she ever asked him for was his love.

Edward Beverly had been first introduced to Lord Mervyn by the Foreign Secretary of the time when he had just supplied him with information regarding a strange man who was suspected of being in league with Russia.

Lord Mervyn was extremely impressed by what he learnt and had persuaded Edward Beverly to accompany him on an expedition that he was making to the north of Africa hoping for a chance to enter Algeria in disguise.

It was on his return from this venture, which was entirely successful, that Edward Beverly was asked to tutor a young man whose father was anxious for him to get a degree before he left Oxford.

He went to stay at Sir Robert Whitehead's magnificent house in Oxfordshire, and he knew as soon as he set eyes on his daughter, Elizabeth, that his wandering days were over.

At the same time he could not be idle and he settled down to write books on the different cultures he had encountered on his travels and to write up his notes on matters that had never been recorded before.

Lord Mervyn, however, refused to accept that Edward Beverly's domestic life should interfere with his plans and after his marriage from time to time he enticed him away from domestic bliss to wild and dangerous missions which might easily have cost him his life.

It was not to say that he did not enjoy them, but because he knew it upset his wife he decided after a second exploration into Algeria, where there had been a strong chance of no return, he had said to his wife:

"I will never leave you again, my darling," as she wept with joy at his safe return.

He had said the same to his fifteen-year-old daughter and meant it.

Now Mrs Beverly thought bitterly that Lord Mervyn was back again to disturb her peace and happiness and make her afraid, even though she told herself not to take seriously Rozella's ridiculous suggestion, of going in her father's place.

"How can she contemplate anything so absurd?" she said aloud.

At that moment Rozella came back into the sitting-room.

She had left it wearing a pretty gown in a shade of green which matched her eyes, but when she returned she was wearing a hideous mackintosh garment that Mrs Beverly recognised as being part of the equipment her husband had used on his travels into the unknown.

It was not merely the clothing she wore on her body that transformed her, but the fact that her face now looked completely different from that of the beautiful girl the sight of whom made every man look and look again.

Over her eyes, which were her most outstanding feature, were tinted spectacles that were used to prevent explorers getting snow-blindness.

Her lovely hair with its strange touches of red that gleamed in the sunshine was shoved away under a hideous mackintosh hat pulled low over her forehead.

She looked, Mrs Beverly had to admit, so nondescript and ordinary, that no one seeing her would give her a second glance.

"Now look at me, Mama!" Rozella said. "If I travel like this to Constantinople, do you really think any man would speak to me, let alone offer to carry my luggage?"

"You are not going to Constantinople!" Mrs Beverly said

with a little tremor in her voice. "And it is no use your trying to persuade me otherwise."

"I intend to go looking like this," Rozella said, "simply because you know as well as I do it will save Papa's life. Are you really prepared to let him die from lack of food and worse still as a result of moving him out of this house?"

Her mother did not reply and after a moment she went on:

"It would make you and me miserable, but it would upset Papa even more because he would be thinking of us rather than of himself. How could we possibly let that happen at this moment? Supposing he dies, what are we going to do then?"

"Oh, Rozella, do not say such things!" Mrs Beverly begged.

"We have to face facts, Mama. We have no money, while like a gift from God five hundred pounds is sitting over there on the table. When that is spent you will have another five hundred pounds which will carry us on very comfortably until Papa is well again."

"I cannot allow you to go into danger," Mrs Beverly pleaded.

"I have the feeling that Lord Mervyn looks after himself quite well. He is not going to lose his life if he can help it and, as he has managed to stay alive so far whatever he has been doing, I see no reason why at Constantinople he should be unsuccessful this time."

"Supposing he does fail?"

"You have to choose, Mama, whether you will risk my going to Constantinople or let Papa lose his life simply through neglect."

"You cannot say such things! You cannot even think about them!" Mrs Beverly protested.

"We have to face the unpalatable truth," Rozella said firmly. "I am not a child any longer. As you know, I am twenty years old and I have always been looked after and

23

cosseted by Papa, you and Nanny."

Rozella paused and then continued:

"However, I really do have a mind of my own and I cannot believe I am so stupid that I cannot find my way to Constantinople. After that Lord Mervyn can look after me."

"And if he refuses?" Mrs Beverly asked.

"That is something he may certainly do,' Rozella said, 'but I have the feeling that when he learns how good I am at languages and that I shall be really useful, he will accept me. Even if he does send me home, we can keep the five hundred pounds!"

"That would be dishonest."

"Not at all! Papa, being himself unable to oblige, has sent him a substitute, and it would be extremely unsporting and ungentlemanly to demand the return of the initial payment even if he may not give us the second five hundred pounds."

"I am not going to let you do this," Mrs Beverly cried.

However the way she spoke told Rozella quite clearly that she knew there was no alternative, and whether she liked it or not and however unhappy it might make her, her daughter must go to Constantinople to save her father's life.

Having once made up her mind that it was the only thing she could do, Rozella wasted no time in further arguments, even though Nanny had even more to say about it than her mother.

She unpacked all her father's special clothes that he had used on his previous expeditions, and found it easy to make herself a skirt out of a cape which, when finished, matched the coat and hat she had put on to show her mother.

These combined with serviceable shoes made her look, when she was finally dressed, like a middle-aged Missionary or one of those faceless English travellers who were to be found in every part of the world.

Apart from the clothes she had from her father, Rozella was forced to pack some clothes of her own.

She could only hope they would sometime serve any purpose that she might require of them.

She had no intention of touching any of the five hundred pounds herself, for that was to save her father's life and bring him back to his full strength.

"What you have to do," she said to Nanny when they were alone, "is to feed everyone until you are all bouncing with health and strength, and even if Lord Mervyn wants some of his money back, he cannot have it because it will already have been eaten!"

Nanny did not reply, but Rozella knew there was a glint in her eyes as if she was already thinking of the delicious dishes she could cook.

Then once again she was giving Rozella a long lecture on the dangers of women moving about the world alone, and how men, all of them, whatever their age, were prowling wolves waiting to devour innocent, shepherdless sheep.

She added also in detail what a mistake it was for women to be mixed up in activities which were essentially masculine.

"I never did approve," Nanny added tartly, "of your father risking his life mixing with those revolutionaries who had nothing better to do than plot against their elders and betters!"

Rozella laughed.

"How do you know that is what he did?"

"I put two and two together," Nanny said, "and I learnt what's what, even if people did try to keep it from me."

Looking back over the years, Rozella found herself remembering some of the things her father had said. They were only scraps of information, but at the same time very revealing.

She knew he had been a spectator of the Dance of the Dervishes, where had any stranger been discovered he would have lost his life.

She knew too that once when he had attempted to reach the most sacred place of all, Mecca, he had only been saved from instant death by being able to run away faster than those who pursued him.

Rozella also remembered that once he had disguised himself as a Fakir and penetrated a camp of tribesmen who were fighting the British.

Because the tribesmen were deceived he had collected a great deal of information which had saved the lives of many soldiers.

"I can hardly expect to do things like that," Rozella told herself sensibly. "At the same time Lord Mervyn would not have sent for Papa unless he knew that he was involved in something very serious."

When she finally said goodbye to her mother, and to Nanny who was weeping copiously, she was carrying with her in a haversack all the notes her father had ever written about the Turks and a selection of books from his extensive library which referred to them.

"At least I shall have some background knowledge about them by the time I get there," she told herself.

With that she set off as a first-class passenger, first on the steamer that crossed the Channel and then in the train she boarded at Calais.

The attendants had looked somewhat surprised and, thinking she was rather unprepossessing to be a first-class passenger, had therefore taken very little notice of her.

Contrary to her expectations, on the train which carried her to Paris where she had changed trains onto the Orient Express, there were no men menacing unattended women.

In fact, her only companions in her carriage were two elderly ladies accompanied by a very old man who had a hacking cough, and who from time to time made them pull his travelling-rug round his knees.

The more she thought about Lord Mervyn the more

Rozella resented the way he had commanded her father's presence as if he were a servant.

She had read the letter several times before she left home and told herself that only an unpleasant and extraordinarily strange type of man would expect anyone to leave his home, wife and daughter, at a moment's notice without one word of regret for the inconvenience caused or even asking him if it was possible for him to do what he asked.

"Papa cannot have any will of his own," she reasoned.

She thought that if Lord Mervyn accepted her to work for him, she would soon show him she was not afraid of him, and she had every intention of impressing her own opinions on him whether he liked it or not.

"Of course he thinks that, because he is important and rich enough to pay for what he wants, he is omnipotent," she thought, "but I intend to make him aware that it is not right or just that any man should play at being God."

Then she laughed because she knew that, if she was honest with herself, she really felt rather frightened at the idea of meeting Lord Mervyn and telling him she had come as a substitute for her father.

Chapter Two

The journey seemed interminable, but at the same time Rozella would have enjoyed it if she had not been apprehensive of what lay ahead.

It was fascinating to travel across Europe seeing countries she had talked about to her father but had never thought she would have an opportunity of actually seeing herself.

When she reached Paris she discovered with tremendous excitement what a first-class ticket on the Orient Express really meant.

Vaguely she could remember her father talking about the Express coming into being in 1889, and she was told when she boarded it that they would reach Constantinople in sixty-seven hours, thirty-five minutes.

Because she had never dreamed that she would ever travel in such luxury she looked around like a child seeing its first Pantomime.

It was not surprising that she was impressed.

The seats had velvet covers topped with Brussels lace and rich damask curtains hung from the windows.

The fittings were of solid oak and mahogany, while hand-cut glass separated the sleeping compartments from the aisle.

In the elegant Saloon cars the diners were offered oysters and chilled glasses of champagne, and were served by attendants in morning-coats, light blue silk breeches, white stockings, and buckled shoes.

Rozella realised how shabby she looked compared with the other female passengers who were all extremely elegant, while the gentlemen, she thought, all looked aristocratic and distinguished.

What she did not realise in her innocence was that attractive *femmes de joie* provided companionship for any lonely male travellers on the long journey to the Orient.

Because she looked so out of place amongst such a well-dressed throng, she was shown to an unobtrusive table for her meals and sat opposite an elderly man who was concerned only with his food.

He did not, in fact, speak one word to her during the whole of the journey.

This actually suited Rozella because she could then look around her and speculate about the other passengers.

She was sure some of the beautiful women dressed in sables and osprey feathers were international spies, and that every man with a fur collar to his coat and an up-turned dashing moustache was an Ambassador whose secrets they were determined to extract from him.

Because she had no one with whom to talk, she made up for herself stories about the various passengers, and thought how amusing it could be if she should discover even more secret and exciting things about them than those Lord Mervyn expected to unearth in Constantinople.

She certainly appreciated the food which was, when they started, the best obtainable in Paris and was supplemented at every station at which they stopped.

When she got out briefly to stretch her legs, as did all the other passengers, she was very careful to keep on her ugly hat and, most important, her tinted spectacles.

There were inevitably on some platforms dashing officers in spectacular uniforms who had, she was sure, a roving eye for a pretty woman.

There were also rather more sinister-looking men, and she wondered if they were in fact the dangerous revolutionaries or anarchists with whom she thought Lord Mervyn and her father had been involved.

The nearer she got to Constantinople, the more she realised how little she knew of what Lord Mervyn expected of her or what in fact he and her father had done together.

She was quite certain it was espionage of some sort, but because her father had always been so reticent in talking of his adventures, she realised how ignorant she was of Lord Mervyn's intentions and that perhaps he would send her back on the next train.

She had been so busy convincing her mother and Nanny that she should go in her father's place, that she had not really worried unduly about Lord Mervyn's probable reaction to her arrival until she had almost reached Constantinople.

Then she sat down to check over in her mind everything she knew about him, which was very little.

One factor, however had made her position worse, she thought, than better. Her mother had said almost casually just before she was leaving:

"One thing, dearest, makes it a little easier for me to let you go."

There had been so many arguments about it that Rozella looked at her in surprise and Mrs Beverly went on:

"Lord Mervyn is a misogynist."

For a moment Rozella could not think what that meant, then she said:

"Do you mean, Mama, that he is a woman-hater?"

"Exactly," Mrs Beverly replied, "and that is why I am not so terrified for you on this mad, crazy adventure as I would be otherwise."

"How do you know that he really hates women?" Rozella asked interestedly.

It was an attitude she had never encountered before, or even heard talked about, with regard to any of the men she had met or her father knew.

"Your father told me about it a long time ago," Mrs Beverly replied. "I was talking about Lord Mervyn and

30

said how much I should like to meet him. Your father laughed. 'I would be jealous of your being interested in a man so much younger than myself,' he said, 'if I was not aware that he is a misogynist.'

"You can imagine," Mrs Beverly went on, "how surprised I was. Then your father told me what I could not help thinking was a rather sad story."

"Tell me, Mama," Rozella begged.

"Well, apparently when Lord Mervyn was still at Oxford, he fell in love with a very attractive girl whose family estate marched with his family's. The parents both of Lord Mervyn – who had not come into the title then – and of the girl thought the match a very suitable one for the reason I have mentioned and because the families had always been very friendly."

Mrs Beverly paused and Rozella asked insistently:

"What happened?"

"As happens so often when it is a question of love," her mother answered, "Lord Mervyn's fiancée fell wildly, head-over-heels, in love with a young man she met out hunting. He was not rich and there was no chance of his coming into a title. She therefore did not dare tell her parents she no longer wished to marry the rich and important young man who lived next door."

"So they ran away!" Rozella exclaimed.

Her mother nodded.

"There was nothing else they could do, and the scandal reverberated through the county. Lord Mervyn was deeply humiliated and, according to your father, he has hated women ever since."

"I suppose one cannot really blame him," Rozella reflected. "It must have been extremely upsetting to learn that the girl he wished to marry had found another man more attractive than he was."

Then as she thought over the story she was sure that, although her father had spoken of Lord Mervyn in glowing

31

terms, it was probable that he was an unattractive man from a woman's point of view.

Knowing her father, she assumed he had been thinking of Lord Mervyn's brains rather than his looks, and admiring his expertise in whatever they were doing rather than being influenced by his personality and, if he had any, his charm.

Thinking of him now, Rozella thought that while her mother was delighted that as a young woman she would not find Lord Mervyn a menace from one point of view, she was certain that as a misogynist he would dislike her on sight and doubtless force her to return to England as quickly as possible.

"In which case I shall not see Turkey," she thought, "nor anything else in this part of the world."

As that was a depressing thought she sent up a little prayer that after all he might find it hard to manage without her.

She wondered how proficient he was in the Turkish language which her father had told her belonged to the Ural-Altaic group and resembled in many of its words the Finnish, Hungarian and Mongolian languages.

This presented little difficulty for Rozella, and she was delighted to think that only fairly recently her father had discussed with her the Kurds in Kurdistan, whose language, though it was much more difficult, she could still understand.

She had also learnt some strange, very rare and difficult dialects spoken in the Eastern Provinces, and of course there had been also infiltrations of Russians over the Caucasus Mountains.

Almost as if she felt Lord Mervyn was already challenging her, Rozella told herself she would not be defeated however difficult his demands might be.

At the same time the last night before she reached Constantinople she prayed very hard that at least Lord Mervyn would let her stay long enough for her to see some of the beauty of a city which had been described as the "pearl of the East".

As she stepped from the train onto Turkish soil the sun was shining on the spires, the domes and the minarets, and however apprehensive she might be, Rozella felt her heart leap with excitement.

She told a porter in his own language to find her a carriage, and thinking she looked of little importance he brought her what she thought was a somewhat dilapidated one with a horse that looked too tired and too underfed move outside the station.

Somehow they set off, and Rozella, wide-eyed, was watching and trying to take in not only the mosques, the palaces, and the fortifications, but the crowded streets with its people of all sorts and different races in national dress.

She noted the street-pedlars, the children, the Muslim women wearing yashmaks and the ugly enveloping burnous, besides what seemed to be an abnormal number of bearded priests and beggars with wasted limbs and crutches.

Then her carriage drew up in front of a very impressive hotel, and she forced herself to control what she knew was a definite fear, and to walk with dignity up to the reception-desk.

She asked for Lord Mervyn and she thought her request seemed to arouse some surprise.

Then a page escorted her up a wide staircase and she followed him, conscious that her ugly, deliberately commonplace clothes made a strange contrast to the elaborate furnishings of what was obviously an expensive hotel.

The page-boy stopped outside a door at the end of a long corridor and knocked, and a sharp, masculine voice called out:

"*Giriniz*!"

Rozella knew this meant "Come In" and the page-boy opened the door.

Now was the moment that she drew in her breath and walked a little taller than she actually was.

She found herself in a large, luxuriously furnished living-room which was obviously intended to be impressive, and she saw seated at a desk in the window a man.

He turned around at her entrance and rose to his feet, but as he had his back to the window she was unable to see him very clearly.

Slowly she walked nearer to him and it was not until she was closer to him that she was aware he was staring at her in surprise. He looked younger and far better-looking than she had expected.

She was however too frightened at that moment to be aware of anything except that he seemed very tall and broad-shouldered, and altogether somewhat overwhelming.

There was silence until he said in English:

"You wished to see me?"

Rozella bobbed him a curtsy.

"I am Rozella Beverly, My Lord, and I have brought you a message from my father."

She thought she saw Lord Mervyn's eyes light up as he said:

"Your father is here? I am expecting him."

"I am afraid, My Lord, you will be disappointed."

"Why? How do you mean disappointed?" Lord Mervyn asked sharply. "Surely if you are here, your father has arrived with you?"

"I am afraid not. My father is in fact very ill and has therefore sent me in his place, knowing that I can do almost anything that you would have required of him."

Lord Mervyn stared at her incredulously.

"I do not understand what you are saying," he said. "Are

34

you telling me that your father cannot carry out my urgent summons to join me here?"

"As I have already said, My Lord, he is ill – very ill indeed – and rather than disappoint Your Lordship he has sent me in his place. I assure you that I can speak any language you require and can help you in any way that my father would have done."

Lord Mervyn walked away across the room to stand in front of the fireplace, almost as if he needed its support behind him.

Then he said:

"I must be very obtuse, but I cannot understand how your father, who I have always considered one of the most intelligent men I have ever met, could imagine for one instant that you could be of the slightest use to me."

He spoke coldly in a domineering tone of voice, but the words did not seem quite as rude as they actually were.

"I was afraid Your Lordship might be a little upset," Rozella said quietly.

"Upset!" Lord Mervyn exclaimed. "I am astonished and find it utterly incredible that your father could be so naïve, for that is the only word I can use, to imagine that a woman could take his place."

Rozella did not speak and he went on:

"It would be hard enough to find anyone approaching your father's calibre and knowledge for what I require, but that he could seriously consider that I could work with a woman makes me feel that he must indeed be very ill, and certainly not – thinking clearly."

There was a pause before the last two words, and Rozella knew Lord Mervyn had intended to say 'not in his right mind'.

She had been standing in the same place as when she had first spoken to him, and now she moved a little nearer to the fireplace to sit down, without being asked to do so, on an upright chair covered in tapestry.

She realised that she had begun a battle with Lord Mervyn, and felt as if her legs would not support her and she needed something more substantial.

Then as she drew in her breath, Lord Mervyn said in a more conciliatory tone:

"I am sure your father thought he was doing his best for me, although it was a very misguided idea, and I suppose, Miss Beverly, I can only thank you for making the journey here and suggest you return after you have had a night's rest."

"I was rather expecting you would say that, My Lord," Rozella said quietly, "but when I told you I could fill my father's place, I was not exaggerating. I imagine you need him because he is fluent in so many languages, and not only speaks in an educated manner, but knows the dialects of the different people with whom you will be associating."

She saw by the expression on Lord Mervyn's face that he did not believe her, and she went on:

"My father has imparted to me over the years a know-ledge of all the people in the countries he has visited, which is much more than the average person learns from history books."

Her voice was impressive as she said: "As I have worked with him so closely I cannot believe you will not find me useful in whatever project you have in mind."

"You are very plausible, Miss Beverly," Lord Mervyn answered, and she thought he was sneering at her. "At the same time you must be aware it would be impossible for any woman to work with me as your father has done."

"I cannot see why," Rozella argued. "Are you not aware that a woman in the East might be able to go into places where a man would not be accepted – a harem for instance – and might be even more sensitive to the complexities of any espionage in which you wished to be involved?"

"Who said I was involved in espionage?" Lord Mervyn asked angrily.

"Perhaps you have a better word for it," Rozella replied, "but my father has told me how grateful the Foreign Office has been in the past for the information you were able to supply to them and which they would have been unable to obtain from other sources."

"Your father had no right to say anything of the sort!" Lord Mervyn snapped.

"He was talking in the past," Rozella said. "After reading the letter you wrote to my father, I cannot help feeling that what you are trying to discover now is the truth about those wild stories you told him were being circulated in this part of the world, and also whether the dark rumours of Russian conspiracy against India as well as other countries in the East are true."

Lord Mervyn's lips tightened as if he was angry she should say such things, but could not contradict them.

After glaring at Rozella in a somewhat ferocious manner which she felt was intended to frighten her, he turned around to look into the fire.

She thought that for the moment he was nonplussed and not quite certain what he should do next.

She had the feeling, and was sure it was true, that he had been counting on her father's co-operation, so that he was now at a loss what to do next and, although he was certain she could be of no assistance, had no idea where else he could look for help.

She did not know how she knew this – it just came into her mind and she was sure it was the truth.

Because it had been some time since Lord Mervyn had moved or spoken, she said:

"I have a suggestion to make, My Lord."

"What is it?"

There was a pause before he answered, as if he had to force himself to speak to her.

"Why," Rozella asked, "do you not give me a chance to prove myself? I have the feeling that what you intended to do with my father was so secret, so confidential, that you have not discussed it with anyone else. My mind is very like his, and because we are so close to each other my mother has often accused us of thinking alike."

She paused and as Lord Mervyn did not turn around or speak she went on:

"Let me try to help you solve your problems. Let me at least justify my father's faith in me by sending me here. Then if you are disappointed I can return as soon as it suits you."

She hoped as she spoke it all sounded very plausible, but was not quite certain whether she could reach through to Lord Mervyn to make him understand.

She was sure he was very hidebound in that he would be completely and absolutely convinced that, apart from his dislike for women as a sex, they were also useless in any activity that did not vitally concern them as females.

She thought she could almost see him thinking that a woman's place was in the kitchen or the nursery, and as far as he was concerned they should never emerge into a world that he considered was specifically masculine and therefore out of bounds for them.

There was what seemed a long silence before Lord Mervyn turned around to say:

"What you suggest is impossible, absolutely impossible! For one thing how am I to explain socially that I am travelling with a woman?"

Because Rozella had been convinced in her own mind that Lord Mervyn's visit to Constantinople was not in any way a social one, this problem had not presented itself to her previously. Now she said quickly:

"I presume no one would be surprised if you had a woman secretary."

"On the contrary, they would be very surprised indeed!" Lord Mervyn said. "And I imagine, since your father is not an old man, you are young enough for it to be extremely difficult for me to explain away your presence."

He peered at her as he spoke, and she thought that under her ugly disguising hat, which she had pulled low over her forehead, it was difficult for him to guess her age or think with her disfiguring spectacles she was anything but an unattractive spinster.

"I suppose," she said after a moment, "that it would be possible to think up some explanation of my being with you without anyone having unpleasant ideas about it."

"Personally I cannot think of any."

Then as if he felt exasperated with the whole thing he exclaimed:

"How could your father have been so absurd, so obtuse, as to think for a moment a woman could help me? The whole thing is preposterous!"

Because his feelings overcame him he walked across the room and stopped at the window to look out over the silver waters of the Golden Horn.

Rozella sat silent and she wondered what more she could say to persuade him that she should stay.

She thought frantically that if he sent her back, as he seemed determined to do, he might demand that his cheque for five hundred pounds should be returned, and there would certainly be no question of a further five hundred.

She thought of her father and how much the money meant at the moment in his precarious state of health, and she knew too that her mother needed good food almost as much as he did.

"I must somehow persuade him," she told herself, and sent up a wild prayer for help that even against his better judgment he might agree to let her stay.

Almost as if her prayer had been answered she heard him say:

"I suppose the only thing I could do is leave here without accepting any of the social invitations which have been pressed upon me, and go direct to Ephesus."

Rozella's eyes widened.

"To Ephesus?" she exclaimed. "Is that where you are intending to go?"

"That is where I have to go!" Lord Mervyn said sharply, as if he resented even having to speak of it to her.

Rozella was surprised. She knew that Ephesus had been one of the great centres of Greek civilisation.

Founded by early Greeks on the coast of Asia Minor, it eventually became the most important city in the Roman Province of Asia, and in the time of St Paul a leading centre of Christianity, and linked especially with Mary, Mother of Jesus.

She was surprised to hear he was going there, and at the same time her heart leapt with the thrill of it.

She told herself it would be a mistake to sound too enthusiastic until Lord Mervyn admitted to himself that it was essential she travelled with him.

She was therefore quiet until he turned around to say:

"If I take you with me temporarily, let me make it quite clear I am doing it only because I am desperate for the help I believed your father would give me. In fact I much resent it that he has sent you in his place instead of finding a young man who would be far more effective."

He was being rude but Rozella knew she had won.

She therefore said quietly:

"Only time can prove how useful I can be to you, and I would like to say that my father knew there was no one more capable than I of taking his place. In any case there was no possible way he could find at a moment's notice, which was all you gave him, someone else."

"It never occurred to me that your father would not be available," Lord Mervyn said, as if he felt he must justify himself.

"Surely it would not be surprising for him to have acquired other interests, considering you have not been in

40

touch with my father for four years."

Lord Mervyn stiffened and said:

"Are you telling me that your father could have come to me, but decided not to do so because he was busy on his own affairs?"

"No, of course not!" Rozella replied. "I am not saying anything like that. All I am saying is it seems extraordinary, My Lord, that you should command – and that is what your letter amounted to – a man of my father's ability and distinction, to leave his home and family at your bidding, without your considering for one moment that, if he had not actually been ill, he might have been deeply engaged in other matters."

She had the satisfaction of knowing that for one moment Lord Mervyn was taken aback.

Then unexpectedly he smiled and it made him look much younger.

"I must admit," he said, "that put in that way, Miss Beverly, my behaviour does sound somewhat arbitrary, but when I wrote immediately before leaving England I was deeply concerned about what I had been asked to do."

He paused before he went on:

"Because your father and I had worked together so amicably in the past, it never struck me for a moment that he might not be willing to assist me once again."

"I am sure that is what Papa would have felt," Rozella said in a slightly more gentle manner, "if he had not been really desperately ill."

"I am very sorry about that," Lord Mervyn said, "but it is something I never expected. What is wrong with him?"

Rozella felt it was something he should have asked before and she replied:

"My father has had a fairly severe heart-attack. He has recovered from it, but at the same time he is very weak and it would be absolutely impossible for him to leave his bed to obey . . . your commands."

41

The last two words were spoken sarcastically and Lord Mervyn gave her a sharp glance before he said:

"I take your point, and of course I am very concerned about him. I sincerely hope he will soon be restored to good health."

Rozella did not speak, she merely inclined her head to show she appreciated his sympathy even if it was somewhat belated, and Lord Mervyn went on:

"Well, now you are here, and I cannot see for the moment what I can do about it, we had better make the best of a bad job."

"That is certainly a very encouraging attitude, My Lord," Rozella replied, and this time there was no doubt of the sarcasm in her voice.

"Damn it all! What do you expect me to feel?" Lord Mervyn asked sharply.

Then as if he realised that in swearing he had been extremely rude he said:

"All right, I apologise, but I should not have spoken so abruptly if you had not faced me with a totally unexpected situation which I am at a loss how to handle."

"Suppose you let things go on naturally as they would have done if my father had joined you," Rozella said. "If the outside world, or social world which concerns you so much, is curious, simply make it quite clear I am taking your secretary's place temporarily, and I cannot believe that if they meet me they would suspect our relationship to be anything else."

As she spoke she thought how wise she had been to disguise herself before she had started the journey, especially now that she realised how much Lord Mervyn disliked and mistrusted women.

Had she not looked so unattractive and of an indeterminate age, he would have sent her packing the first moment he had set eyes on her.

"I must be very careful," Rozella thought, "not to let

him see me any other way."

That might be difficult, but at the same time she thought how clever she had been to ensure she was not embarrassed in any way on the journey, even though she had travelled alone.

None of the passengers, none of the dashing soldiers she had seen on the platforms, had given her a second glance.

She was not so foolish as not to realise everything would have been very different, however unbecomingly or poorly dressed she had been, if she had appeared without her father's ugly coat which Nanny had altered to fit her, her spectacles, and of course her quite appalling rain-proof hat.

"Well, we must make the best of things," Lord Mervyn said in a brisk manner. "I will send for a page-boy to show you to the bedroom I had engaged for your father, and you can tell him to bring up your luggage. Do not unpack much, only what is completely necessary, as we shall not be staying here long. When you are ready I would like to discuss the situation here and tell you a little of what we are up against."

Rozella drew in her breath and knew this was exactly what she wanted to hear.

"Thank you," she said, "and now if I can just wash my hands and tidy myself, I am very anxious to hear anything Your Lordship desires to impart to me."

As she rose to her feet, Lord Mervyn said as if he was talking to himself:

"I suppose I am doing the only possible thing, but I am frightened, extremely frightened, Miss Beverly, that you may mess up all my plans."

"I will do my very best not to," Rozella replied. "I cannot say more."

"You do realise, but I expect your father has told you, that here, as in other places in the world where we have worked together, we walk a tight-rope. Any unwary move, any unfortunate slip of the tongue, could mean that one or

43

both of us might have what is known as an 'unfortunate accident', in which case we should not return home."

Lord Mervyn spoke so seriously that Rozella felt a little tremor of fear.

It was no more than she had expected, but at the same time to think she might be frightened of what might happen, was very different from feeling fear flickering through her like a streak of forked lightning.

She felt however there was nothing she could say, and as Lord Mervyn put out his hand to ring the bell for the page-boy, she said:

"Will we be travelling alone?"

"My valet will be with me, a man who is completely and utterly trustworthy," Lord Mervyn said. "I am surprised your father did not tell you about him. He always thought he was quite a character."

Looking back Rozella could not remember her father mentioning the man in question, and she knew that another of her problems would be not to let Lord Mervyn know that her father actually had no idea where she was at the moment.

She had asked her mother if they should tell him what she intended to do, and Mrs Beverly had exclaimed in horror at the idea.

"Your father would worry in a way that would be extremely bad for him," she had said, "if he had the slightest idea you were attempting anything so outrageous as to go to Lord Mervyn. In fact he would refuse point blank to let you do so."

Rozella thought this was more than likely, and she therefore intrigued with her mother to make quite certain her father was not in the least suspicious when she told him she was going to stay with one of her friends.

She knew he was surprised since having very few friends in the neighbourhood she never went away.

However she told him that since he had been ill she had

become very fond of a young girl she had met once or twice who lived about fifteen miles away, and whom he was extremely unlikely to meet by accident in her absence.

"They have asked me to stay with them for a small party they are giving," she said, "which Mama thought would be a nice change for me, and they are also having a Point-to-Point which she thinks I would like to watch as her brother is taking part in it."

"I am sure you will enjoy it," her father had said weakly. "Your mother tells me how wonderful you have been while I have been so ill."

He smiled and then added:

"Do not stay away too long, my lovely daughter. I like having you with me and looking at you, even if I cannot talk as much as I usually do."

"You will soon be talking again nineteen-to-the-dozen," Rozella had laughed, "and do not forget, Papa, that you have a lot of work to catch up with for your new book. At the moment we have stopped at Chapter Four and I am really excited about what comes next."

Her father had put out his hand to hold hers.

"You encourage me, dearest, even though I think you are perhaps the only reader I have."

"Nonsense," Rozella had replied, "and I have a feeling that this book will be the best you have ever done!"

She bent down to kiss him.

"Hurry up and get well, Papa. Not only Mama and I need you, but so does your public."

He had laughed at that as she had meant him to, and she had known when she left home he would not really miss her as much as he said because he was always so happy with her mother.

"Everything will be different now they have good food to eat, and if Papa falls ill again we can afford to call in a specialist," she told herself.

But everything had depended on her being accepted by

Lord Mervyn, and now he had done so, even though grudgingly, she suddenly felt weak after having fought him not only with her words and her mind, but with her very heart and soul.

'I have won! I have won!' she thought as the page-boy who had answered Lord Mervyn's summons led her further along the passage to where the bedroom reserved for her father was only a few doors from Lord Mervyn's suite.

It was a comfortable room. Her luggage had already been brought upstairs and when she tipped the page he said with a wink:

"I hopes you enjoys yourself, Miss."

He did not wait for her reply, and as the door closed behind him, Rozella sat down limply on the side of the bed and pulled off first her glasses and then her ugly shapeless hat.

She had a glimpse of herself in the mirror on the other side of the room, and as the sun coming through the window illuminated her hair, making the red streaks in it shimmer like little tongues of fire, she told herself again she must be very careful.

It was not going to be easy to prevent Lord Mervyn from seeing her as she was, but she knew, now she had met him, it was absolutely essential.

"If he dislikes me as a woman when I look like a middle-aged missionary," she told herself, "what will he feel if he sees me looking like myself?"

Chapter Three

Rozella was not surprised when it was luncheon-time to find the food being brought to her bedroom.

It was wheeled in on a trolley-table and elegantly served and she would have appreciated the delicious dishes even more if she had not already enjoyed so much good food on the Orient Express.

She was sure the food she had eaten between Paris and Constantinople had already improved her appearance and made her feel better than she had for a long time.

At every meal she had found herself wishing that her mother and father could be with her so that they could eat as well as she was.

Then she remembered that the £500 from Lord Mervyn would immeasurably have improved the food at home, and she told herself whatever rudeness and antagonism she had to put up with from him, it was worth it to know that her father would be growing stronger day by day.

When she had finished luncheon the table was taken away by a polite waiter, and after he had gone a knock came at the door.

As soon as she saw the small man standing there she knew before he spoke that he was Lord Mervyn's valet.

" 'Mornin', Miss!" he said politely.

She was aware that his shrewd eyes were looking over her speculatively as he took in every detail of her appearance and was making up his own mind as to what he thought of her.

"Good-morning!" Rozella replied questioningly, waiting for him to introduce himself.

"I'm His Lordship's valet, Miss," he explained as if she had asked the question aloud. "Hunt's my name, and I'm real sorry to hear as how your father's been taken ill."

"Yes, he has had a heart-attack," Rozella replied.

"I'm sorry about that, Miss. We'll miss him."

Rozella smiled.

"I am hoping not as much as if he had not sent me to take his place."

She was deliberately being charming, feeling it was very important that she should get the third member of the party on her side.

To her relief Hunt grinned back at her.

"You gave his Lordship a real shock, Miss, turning up like that!" he said. "If you wants the truth, it was a surprise to me he didn't send you back as quick as you came!"

"I am very afraid he may do that anyway," Rozella replied, "so I am hoping, Mr Hunt, that you will help me to do what His Lordship wants and not make too many mistakes."

Hunt laughed before he answered:

"Well, that's asking a lot, seeing as how no one could expect you to be as clever as the Professor."

"I agree with you," Rozella smiled, "at the same time, he has taught me all the languages he knows himself, and I know I can help His Lordship in that way, if in no other."

"You're still going to have to prove yourself, Miss."

"In what way?" Rozella asked.

"His Lordship's got two visitors coming here at about four o'clock. He wants to see you before they arrives."

Hunt pulled his watch out of his waistcoat-pocket and added:

"That'll be in about an hour-and-a-half. I expect you can find something to do 'til His Lordship wants you?"

"What I would like to do," Rozella said quickly, "if it is no trouble, is to have a chance of getting a little fresh air. I have been cooped up in the train, as you know, for the last few days, and I am also longing to see Constantinople."

There was a pause. Then as she had hoped, Hunt said:

"Well, I've got nothing to do for an hour or so, if you'd like me to come with you."

"I would love it!" Rozella said eagerly.

"I'll give you five minutes, Miss," Hunt said, "and I'll wait for you downstairs."

Rozella gave a cry of delight, and as he shut the door she hurried to put on the ugly coat she had discarded while she had her meal.

She had been careful not to remove her hat, and she had been thinking during luncheon how she could continue to disguise her hair if Lord Mervyn sent for her.

At the moment it was easy to wear the hat made of mackintosh which she had worn all the time she was on the Orient Express.

She was certain now she had seen Lord Mervyn that it was more important even than it had been on the train to keep up the disguise of being a nondescript figure of uncertain age who would not intrude in any way upon his thoughts.

Hunt was waiting for her in the large marble hall, and she ran excitedly down the stairs thinking as she did so that her mother would be horrified at the idea of her setting out on a voyage of discovery with a valet.

At the same time, she knew that the only way to see anything she really wanted to see would be with Hunt, for she was quite certain that His Lordship would have no intention of squiring her anywhere.

The next hour was one of sheer delight.

Hunt pointed out to her the great dome and four spiral minarets of Santa Sophia, the most famous mosque in the whole of Turkey.

He also showed her the Galata Bridge over the Golden Horn, then to her delight, took her to the Spice Bazaar which was near it.

49

In the garden outside she was fascinated by the people who had come here to buy plants and sit about staring at each other.

She saw a man selling leeches from a bottle, and another who held up pieces of mandrake root which he said would magic away rheumatism.

Hunt insisted that she should have her fortune told by a pigeon who would pick out a piece of paper for her.

"I cannot waste my money on such nonsense!" Rozella protested.

"I'll treat you, Miss!" Hunt said.

The pigeon obliged and Rozella took the small piece of paper from his beak, opened it and read in Turkish:

"You will battle and win – so fight on!"

She laughed as she showed it to Hunt and he said:

"If that refers to your battle with His Lordship, I think I ought to warn you he's always victorious!"

"I was not in fact thinking of His Lordship," Rozella replied, "although perhaps it would be very good for him to lose for a change, even if it only meant a slight retreat."

Hunt shook his head.

"I'm warning you, Miss, he's never the loser," he said, "it's always the other fellow who bites the dust!"

Rozella laughed again and said:

"I think, Mr Hunt, you are trying to frighten me."

"As it happens, I'm telling you the truth," he replied, "but you're a woman, and you can never tell with a woman what'll turn up!"

Rozella thought it would be a mistake to go on talking about herself and quickly changed the subject.

There was so much to see, so much to stare at in the crowded bazaar.

Rozella was entranced by sacks of cardamom, coriander and cumin. The sharp scent of pepper and aromatic fragrance of cloves mingled with the rich red-gold strength of turmeric.

The time Hunt had allotted her seemed to pass by in a few minutes before they walked back towards the hotel.

As they reached it Rozella said:

"What shall I do now?"

"Sit in your room, Miss and wait for His Lordship's summons. I don't suppose it'll be long before I comes to fetch you to his Sitting-Room."

Rozella looked at him, then she said:

"I expect His Lordship will ask you to give a report on me. Be kind! Remember, if he sends me home, my father will be very hurt at my having failed, and I expect I shall have an inferiority complex about it for the rest of my life!"

"How did you know that's what His Lordship'll ask me?" Hunt enquired.

"I know that is the sort of thing both Papa and His Lordship would ask about anybody who joined their party, and they would trust you to find out the worst about them."

Hunt laughed at this. Then he said:

"You're too shrewd, Miss, that's what's the matter with you! Just you be careful and watch your step, and I'm certain His Lordship'll be happy to keep you with us 'til the Professor's better."

"Thank you for giving me hope, and thank you too for showing me so much," Rozella said. "I have enjoyed every minute of it."

"So have I, now I comes to think of it!" he said.

She was laughing as she went up the stairs, and as she reached her bedroom she was hoping that she had Hunt on her side.

If nothing else, he would not recommend to Lord Mervyn to get rid of her at once as she had feared.

She thought however that her mother might be shocked at her for being so familiar with a valet.

At the same time, she was sure that Hunt was different from the ordinary type of servant whom she would meet in any Gentleman's house.

For one thing, he was obviously in his master's confidence. For another, if he was clever enough to have travelled with Lord Mervyn and her father on their expeditions, he must be a master of disguise as they were.

He would therefore, be clever enough to deceive the ordinary people amongst whom they moved, who had no idea of who they really were or what was their position in life.

Because she had been determined from the moment she saw him to make sure of his co-operation where she was concerned, she had deliberately addressed him as 'Mr.'

She guessed that he would appreciate the subtle difference from calling him simply by his surname, as his employer and her father would have done.

She had noticed too that he spoke Turkish well, and she had the idea that he might well have mastered a great number of other languages.

When she was in her bedroom however she did not go on thinking about Hunt, but of what she should wear when Lord Mervyn sent for her.

As she had thought at luncheon, she could hardly go on wearing her father's hat.

When she took it off in front of the mirror and saw the sun shining on her red-gold hair, she knew that if she did not manage to do something about her appearance, Lord Mervyn would dislike her more than he did already.

She had brought in her luggage from England several articles which she expected to find useful in the art of disguise.

She thought as she picked up a large silk handkerchief which had belonged to her father and which was a rather ugly shade of blue, that it was not often that an attractive young woman was forced into disguising herself as somebody elderly and unprepossessing.

However, by the time she had covered her hair completely with the silk handkerchief, tying it across her forehead and at the back of her neck, pirate-fashion, there was not a vestige of her hair to be seen, and her large tinted spectacles made her, with her thin face, look rather like an owl.

It was obviously impossible in the late afternoon when it was quite warm to go on wearing her father's coat which Nanny had altered for her. The sleeves were shorter but it still enveloped her in something like a barrel-shaped cocoon.

She therefore had to decide what else she could put on.

She was thinking all the time she was changing one of the blouses that were of a cheap material but skilfully made either by her mother or Nanny who were both excellent needle-women.

They would not have impressed another woman as being particularly smart, but, as Rozella was aware, they revealed the curves of her breasts and tucked into the belt of her skirt made her waist look very small.

"I must wear something over my shoulders," she decided.

She had the choice of either a long, heavy wool coat which her father had worn in the mountains when it was very cold, or a grey shawl that she had borrowed from Nanny.

She decided on the latter, and crossed it demurely over her breasts. Looking at herself in the mirror she thought she was actually almost a figure of fun.

At the same time, she might have been any age, and her appearance certainly had nothing about it to make a man even conscious that she was a woman.

She then sat down in the window and read with interest the Turkish newspaper she had bought when out with Hunt.

It told her very little that she wanted to know about the situation in Turkey at the moment. At the same time, she was delighted to find that she could read it without any difficulty.

She was just coming to the end of the leading article when a tap on the door made her aware that her summons had come.

When she opened the door Hunt said:

"His Lordship's waiting for you, Miss, an' I warns you, if you want to stay, this is important!"

"Thank you for the warning," Rozella replied, "and if you have nothing better to do, you might send up a prayer that I shall not be knocked out in the first round."

Hunt grinned at this.

Then as if he reverted to his position as a servant, he went ahead of her and opening the door of the Sitting-Room he announced in a respectful tone:

"Miss Beverly, M'Lord!"

Lord Mervyn was sitting at the desk and he made a very slight movement as if to rise as Rozella entered, then sat down again.

She walked forward and as she stood opposite him he said sharply:

"Sit down, Miss Beverly. I have quite a lot to say to you, and there is not much time."

"I am listening, My Lord," Rozella said politely.

"I suppose you have some idea, or perhaps your father will have told you, of the situation in Turkey at the moment?"

"I know a little," Rozella replied, "but I would like to know a great deal more."

She was not certain whether Lord Mervyn gave a sigh of exasperation, or whether he just took a deep breath.

Then he said:

"I am sure you are aware that Turkey was making a rapid advance towards democracy, when the brake was applied

54

to any reform by the suspicious and reactionary Abdul-Hamid II who is now the Sultan."

"Yes, my father told me that."

"Reform was therefore forced underground," Lord Mervyn went on. "A Secret Society of New Ottomans was formed here in Constantinople and, although it was disbanded, its members have continued the reformist struggle."

Rozella nodded to show that she was also aware of this and Lord Mervyn continued:

"It is very important from the point of view of the Great Powers that Turkey should not be as closely identified with Russia as it appears to be at the moment. As I am sure you are well aware, Russia is a 'thorn in the flesh' of Britain when it comes to the question of India and Afghanistan."

He spoke briskly and crisply as if he resented having to give such information away, even though so far he had said nothing of which Rozella was not aware.

"The true picture," he said after a slight pause, "is too complicated to explain in a few words, but your father knows that the Armenians are in revolt entirely owing both to the Sultan's foolish patronage of the Kurds which has encouraged them to persecute the Armenians, and to the severity with which the taxes are collected."

Rozella did not speak and after a little pause Lord Mervyn sat looking at her speculatively as if to judge her reactions before he continued:

"Lastly, our Minister here, Sir Philip Currie, has repeated to me what we have already heard in England, that the Russians have said openly that their mission in Asia is to destroy British rule in India."

He paused before he went on:

"All these things, although it may not be at all obvious, are linked together, and their repercussions and a number of other factors as well are what I had hoped your father would help me unearth and transmit back to London."

There was a short pause before Rozella said quietly:

"I am here to take my father's place, and I hope I may be able to help you."

Lord Mervyn leant forward, then he said:

"I have coming here in a very short time, Miss Beverly, two people who have expressed themselves as being very anxious to be friendly and to entertain me in every possible manner since I came to the city. One of them is an important Turk called Ali Pasha who is in a position to exercise great influence with the Sultan and, I think, with most of the Ministers."

He paused before he continued:

"The other is a relative of his, a very attractive woman whom I have met on a number of occasions in the past, and who has made it clear that she wishes my visit to Turkey to be a very enjoyable one."

The way Lord Mervyn spoke was cold and constrained and yet Rozella felt she could read something intimate into his words.

"What I am going to say," he went on, "is that I would like to have your opinion on both these people, who while they are here, will not be aware that you are listening to what they are saying."

Rozella felt her eyes twinkling. She knew now what Lord Mervyn wanted.

"What you are asking, My Lord," she said, "is that I should spy on them. But how?"

"That is a question I was going to ask you," he replied. "You see this room? Tell me where you think you could conceal yourself without it being obvious, or likely to arouse suspicion."

Rozella looked around the square, ornately furnished room and knew this was a rather difficult question.

There was no screen, no cupboards, except for two glass-fronted bookcases, the shelves of which also displayed china.

Otherwise, there were just sofas and chairs covered with heavy velvet resting on a rich, elaborately patterned carpet.

Automatically her eyes went towards the windows which almost filled one wall and which had curtains also of heavy velvet, braided and tasselled, as was fashionable not only abroad but in most houses at home.

Lord Mervyn followed the direction of her eyes and said:

"That seems to be our only choice. By the time my guests arrive it will be growing dark, and they will therefore not be particularly surprised if the curtains are already closed."

Rozella was about to acquiesce, then she said:

"May I make a suggestion, My Lord?"

"Of course!"

"I think if I were shown into a room where the curtains were closed rather earlier in the evening than was necessary, I would be suspicious."

For a moment he stiffened, almost as if she had accused him of being impractical in his planning.

Quickly Rozella went on:

"If I might suggest it, My Lord, I think it would be far more subtle if the curtains were partly drawn forward on each side. Your valet could show your guests into the room, and as he does so you could say to him:

'Draw the curtains, Hunt, and light the lamps!' '

There was a pause while Lord Mervyn considered her suggestion. Then thinking it an intelligent one, he said:

"Very well, Miss Beverly, I agree to what you say, and I will make sure that Hunt and not one of the hotel servants escorts my guests here."

As he spoke he rang the bell on the desk and as Hunt appeared at the door immediately, Rozella knew he had been waiting outside and, if possible, listening.

Lord Mervyn gave him his instructions and she went across the room to stand in a corner of the window squeezed against the wall with the heavy velvet curtains in front of her.

Lord Mervyn adjusted them so that they fell a good two-and-a-half feet from each side of the window, still leaving a large area of glass uncovered in the centre.

Having satisfied himself that they hung naturally, it was only as he turned to go back to the desk that he asked:

"You are quite comfortable, Miss Beverly?"

"Quite comfortable, thank you, My Lord."

"You do realise that if my guests have the slightest suspicion that you are there, the result could be disastrous for both of us?"

"I understand, My Lord!"

He gave her a sharp glance as if he were not really satisfied with her answer, then he walked back to his desk and Rozella heard him sit down at it.

She leant back against the wall, feeling as if she were taking part in some childish game.

But she knew at the same time that what she was doing was very serious and, as Lord Mervyn had said, were she to be discovered or he accused of placing her in such a position, it would be disastrous not only for them, but perhaps also for Turkish relations with Great Britain.

Now feeling very nervous, she sent up a prayer that everything would go well and she would not fail in what she had to do.

She thought of her father and how he would act in the same conditions.

Then as if her thoughts were interrupted almost by a trumpet-call, she heard the door open and Hunt announce Lord Mervyn's guests.

She could hear Lord Mervyn pushing back his chair as he rose to his feet to exclaim:

"How delightful to see you!"

Rozella listening felt he was walking towards them as he said:

"Close the curtains, Hunt, and light the lamps."

"Very good, M'Lord!"

There was a number of greetings volubly expressed by Lord Mervyn's visitors which to Rozella's surprise were spoken in English.

This was something she had not expected, and while she knew the Turkish man spoke quite well, he made many mistakes and had a distinct accent.

On the other hand the woman, whom she had heard called Princess Eudocia, spoke more fluently but surprisingly with a French accent.

There was no doubt from the way she was speaking beguilingly and at the same time flirtatiously to Lord Mervyn what she felt about him.

She was telling him about a special party she was giving the next night, and in almost the same breath inviting him to honour her by attending a quiet dinner that evening when they could talk of many things which it would be impossible to do at the party.

Listening, Rozella thought with amusement that she was certainly setting out to enslave Lord Mervyn, and she wondered how he would react to such blandishments.

After they had chatted together for nearly twenty minutes Lord Mervyn said:

"By the way, I have some presents which I brought out with me from England but which I have not had a chance to give you until now."

There was a pause as if he was looking around for them. Then he said:

"I told my servant to bring them in here, but he must have left them in my bedroom. If you will excuse me for a moment I will fetch them for you."

"Presents!" the Princess exclaimed. "How delightful! And how kind of you to think of it!"

Rozella heard Lord Mervyn rise from wherever he was sitting and walk across the room to pass through the communicating-door which led into his bedroom.

He shut the door behind him almost noisily.

There was a short silence before the Princess said in a low voice little above a whisper:

"It is hopeless, and you were quite right, he is not interested in women!"

She was speaking in Turkish, and the man replied:

"How can you be sure?"

"How could I not be sure?" she answered. "Those cold English eyes, the stiffness of his back, and his frigid handshake like ice! *Mon Cher*, he is frozen! How can I melt an icicle?"

"You have to try, Eudocia," the man insisted. "It is important, as you know, and who else can we trust who is on the same footing with him as we are?"

"I tell you it is impossible!" the Princess said.

"Well, try tonight. Can you not put into his food or drink a little . . . ?"

The man had dropped his voice so low that it was impossible for Rozella to hear what he said.

Then the Princess exclaimed:

"That is clever of you! Why did I not think of that? But of course, if it is dissolved in a good red wine, it is impossible for anybody to detect it."

"That is true."

"Then I must make sure that he has dinner with me as I have asked him to do."

As she finished speaking the communicating-door opened and Lord Mervyn came back into the room.

Rozella knew he had with him the presents of which he had spoken, for there were cries of delight from both his guests, and the Princess said:

"How can I thank you for thinking of me except by making sure that we have the most delectable dinner tonight that has ever been devised for a most generous and at the same time, most magnificent man?"

"You are flattering me," Lord Mervyn replied, "and I

need no reward for having pleased you."

"Unfortunately, we must go now," the Princess said rising to her feet, "but I shall look forward and indeed shall be counting the minutes, until we meet again at my house at eight o'clock this evening."

Lord Mervyn did not reply instantly and she added quickly, almost as if she was afraid he was thinking it over:

"I shall have one of the most interesting and intelligent men in Turkey to meet you. I shall not now tell you his name for it is to be a surprise. If you do not come I know he will be disappointed, as I shall be."

"Then I must do my best to be there," Lord Mervyn said, "and I can assure Your Highness you have made me very curious as to what this evening will hold for me."

"I am hoping," the Princess replied, "that it will mean a few hours of pleasure and Eastern delights that will be different from anything you have ever experienced in London."

"As you can imagine, I am very intrigued."

Rozella listening was sure that he now kissed the Princess's hand.

Then there were the usual genial goodbyes and Rozella knew that Lord Mervyn was accompanying them to the top of the stairs where Hunt was waiting to take them down into the vestibule and see them into their carriage.

Lord Mervyn stood watching until they were out of sight, but Rozella did not move from where she was hiding, knowing it was always a mistake to come from any place of concealment until there was no possibility of being discovered.

She had to be sure that those upon whom she had been spying had no chance of coming back and finding her in the room.

Finally, however, she heard Lord Mervyn come into the Sitting-Room, shut the door and, she thought, lock it.

Then he said:

"You can come out now, Miss Beverly!"

She moved from behind the heavy velvet curtains into the room which was golden with the light from the lamps.

Lord Mervyn was sitting once again at his desk.

She walked towards him thinking that he glanced at her, then quickly looked away as if in contrast to the Princess she looked very unprepossessing, and so plain as not to be compared with her.

He did not speak and she stood in front of the desk waiting for him to raise his head from the notes he was writing.

When he did so she had the impression that he was resenting having to rely on her for an opinion, and was in consequence regretting that he had set a trap for his visitors.

At last he asked:

"Well?"

It was an uncompromising question.

"May I sit down?" Rozella asked. "I have been standing for rather a long time."

For a moment Lord Mervyn glared at her because he knew she was in fact, rebuking him.

Then he said:

"I apologise. Of course sit down, Miss Beverly, and tell me what you overheard."

She started to repeat word for word the conversation to which she had listened, but he interrupted to ask:

"What language were they speaking?"

"Turkish, although the Princess has a French accent when she is speaking English."

"That is perceptive of you," Lord Mervyn remarked. "The Princess has in fact lived in Paris for some years as her husband was attached to the Turkish Embassy there. She assisted him to get information by having a great number of lovers who revealed or so I have always understood many of the secrets he wished to know."

As if he was suddenly aware that he was speaking to a woman on a somewhat embarrassing subject he said sharply:

"Go on with what you were telling me."

He did not interrupt again, and when Rozella had finished he said slowly:

"Then they intend to use a drug on me!"

"I . . . I am afraid I could not hear its name."

"I know exactly what it is. It is a drug well known in the East, especially in this country."

"It is very potent?"

"Very, if given in large doses."

"Do you mean that it will make you talkative?"

There was a twist to Lord Mervyn's lips before he replied:

"It will also make me very susceptible to anything the Princess suggests. Perhaps that is something I should not say to you, Miss Beverly, but as you came in your father's place, it is difficult not to speak frankly, despite the fact you are a woman."

"I understand it is embarrassing for you, My Lord," Rozella said. "At the same time, I think if we are to work together, as I hope, it would be better if you put aside any scruples as regards my being shocked or expecting deferential treatment because I am supposed to be a Lady."

She thought there was a faint smile at the corners of Lord Mervyn's mouth as she continued:

"Just make an effort, My Lord, to think of me as being my father, rather than myself. He always says that the great art of disguise is to 'think' one's-self into the part. If that is possible, why should you not think of me either as my father, or else as the son he never had, in which case there would be no reason for you to feel either constrained or embarrassed."

"I understand your reasoning, Miss Beverly," Lord Mervyn replied, "and I will certainly bear it in mind. In the meantime, thank you for your help."

He paused before he added:

"Perhaps I should apologise for not expecting your father's daughter to be quite so efficient and able to repeat so fluently what was said in a different language from your own."

Chapter Four

Lord Mervyn arrived at the house of Princess Eudocia at eight o'clock.

As he expected, she was waiting for him in a large be-flowered and perfumed room, looking extremely seductive in a gown which had 'Paris' written all over it.

She was a beautiful woman and had been acclaimed ever since she had been married at the age of fifteen to Prince Nyssa Sokolla, who was already noted as an up and coming Diplomat.

When, after some years of moving around the Capitals of Europe they were posted to Paris, the Princess became a success overnight, and her beauty was acclaimed even by the ultra-fastidious Parisians.

It would have been impossible for any man not to appreciate her large dark eyes fringed with black lashes, her magnolia skin and provocatively curved lips.

But the expression on Lord Mervyn's face did not alter as he kissed her hand.

"It is wonderful that you could come," the Princess said in a soft voice, and he was conscious as she spoke that she moved a little nearer to him.

He thought the exotic scent of her perfume was an invitation in itself.

Standing beside her was a tall, distinguished-looking man whom she introduced as Ali Pasha, but addressed as Petrus.

Lord Mervyn knew at once that he was a man he had wanted to meet for some time, and whose name was already in one of the most secret files of the Foreign Office in London.

It was suspected that his interests, like the Sultan's, were with the Kurds, and there was also a vague reference to some involvement in Afghanistan which was however not proven.

There was champagne to drink before dinner and Lord Mervyn was careful, even though it was the red wine of which Rozella had warned him, to note that Ali Pasha and the Princess lifted their glasses from the silver salver on which it was proffered without appearing to concentrate on which they were taking.

His years of espionage had taught him to make note of every single little detail, and when he was on a mission he was aware that even a slight flicker of an eye-lid or a movement of a little finger might have some significance.

After they had drunk quite a considerable amount of champagne in the Princess's Drawing-Room, they moved into the Dining-Room which Lord Mervyn found attractively furnished in French rather than Turkish taste.

The food they were served was delicious and could only have been prepared by a French chef.

He was however concentrating more on the conversation than on what he was eating, and he found Ali Pasha was witty and extremely astute in introducing subjects in which he himself was interested and on which Lord Mervyn knew he wished to hear his opinion.

They talked of the wild rumours that were being circulated about the Moslem unrest and Ali Pasha said disarmingly:

"You must be aware, Lord Mervyn, that my people are fighting a losing battle in that they can see the great Ottoman Empire crumbling and are making an effort to prop it up with both words and actions."

"I can understand that," Lord Mervyn said. "At the same time rumours of that sort which in many instances are palpably untrue, have a habit of boomeranging on those who invented them!"

Ali Pasha laughed before he said:

"And what do you make, My Lord, of the story that a Holy Man known to the British as 'the Mad Fakir' has succeeded in inciting the tribesmen in the North of India to a rebellion which may eventually drive the British out?"

Lord Mervyn had already heard of the Mad Fakir, and he knew that the man, who was revered by the tribesmen, had succeeded in making those on the North-West Frontier more restless and aggressive than usual.

The British authorities were almost convinced that the Mad Fakir himself had been indoctrinated by the Russians, who were supplying the tribesmen with weapons to use against their British overlords.

They were at the same time attempting to make trouble in Afghanistan.

Aloud however he said:

"There have always been Fakirs who preach sedition, as I found when I was in India. But tell me about this one, because I do not think I have heard of him before."

He knew as he spoke that Ali Pasha did not believe him.

Instead he started on another tack, to relate how the *Mahdi*, ten years after defeating General Gordon and forcing the British to evacuate the Sudan, was still conducting frontier warfare against them and had claimed the faithful could never be hurt by British bullets.

He was said to display a mild bruise on his own leg which he said was the only result of a direct hit from a 12-lb shell.

At this story Lord Mervyn laughed heartily and said:

"What a pity it is that the British could not reply with a four-leaf clover, or perhaps some sacred emblem which would render them immune from the poisoned spears of the Mahdi's followers!"

As the evening passed, both men realised they were fencing with each other and finding it most enjoyable.

But they also talked more seriously of Turkish interests in Greece, and the difficulties in Kurdistan.

While they were talking, course succeeded course, and Lord Mervyn was not surprised when, after some excellent white wine which accompanied the fish, a claret was produced to go with the *Kebab*.

A dish that was famous the length and breadth of Turkey, it consisted of small pieces of tender baby lamb, pierced on a skewer and interspersed with tomatoes and cooked over a charcoal fire. It both looked and tasted delicious.

He noticed however, without giving any sign of doing so, that the decanter from which his glass of claret was poured was different from the one used for the Princess and Ali Pasha.

He ate his *Kebab* and left his claret untouched until the Princess bending forward seductively said:

"I think, dear Lord Mervyn, that I must drink a toast to you as a very favoured guest, whom I have wanted for a long time to entertain here in Constantinople."

"You are most gracious," Lord Mervyn replied, "and of course I shall be very honoured to drink a toast to not only the most beautiful woman in Turkey, but one who shone like a star in Paris."

"And in every part of the world she has ever visited!" Ali Pasha added flatteringly.

"But first I must drink to you," the Princess insisted to Lord Mervyn, "and you, Petrus, must join me."

"Of course!" the Turk replied, "and I cannot adequately express, My Lord, what an admiration I have for you, and my hope in the future to be able to value your friendship."

"You are very kind," Lord Mervyn smiled.

The Princess and Ali Pasha raised their glasses and drank to him.

Then as he knew this was the moment in which he had to reply he rose unexpectedly to his feet.

The servants had left the room after serving each course, and he knew this was quite usual in the East where it was always unwise for anyone, if they had anything to hide, to speak in front of the servants, however much they trusted them.

They were therefore alone in the room and Lord Mervyn, holding his glass in his hand, made a short, witty and amusing speech extolling the beauty of his hostess and praising Ali Pasha as being one of the most astute brains in the whole of the Ottoman Empire.

It was obvious that both his listeners were very gratified.

Then as he raised his glass to the Princess saying: "To my hostess and to her brilliant guest!" he loosened the gold signet-ring which he wore on his little finger so that it fell with a tinkling crash onto the table.

It rolled over the polished surface towards the orchids which decorated a gold vase in the centre of it.

In the split second in which the Princess and Ali Pasha were watching its progress, Lord Mervyn bent forward and downward, stretching out his left hand to pick up his ring and emptied the glass of claret in his other hand onto the floor.

He was careful in doing so that the fingers of his right hand encircled the wine glass so that it was impossible for anybody to see that it was in fact empty.

Holding it high above their heads he said:

"After that slight interruption, let me complete my toast to you both. May the future bring you everything you want and desire, and above all things, happiness!"

As he finished speaking he appeared to tip the contents of his glass down his throat.

Then as he sat down again putting his empty glass on the table in front of him, the Princess clapped her hands.

"That was a lovely toast, My Lord, and I am deeply touched by the flattering things you have said to me, as I am sure Petrus is."

She rang a bell and the servants entered instantly to clear away the empty dishes and bring in a sorbet, which was followed by *crêpes suzettes* cooked with the light touch and expertise that could only be achieved by the French.

With these two last courses there was champagne to drink as Lord Mervyn expected, but almost before he had finished his *crêpes suzettes* his elbow was on the table and he was supporting his head with his hand as if he was finding it hard to keep awake.

In fact while he was talking his voice frequently trailed away into a mere murmur.

He knew that Ali Pasha was looking knowingly at the Princess until finally she said:

"I think we should move into the Drawing-Room, and I have no intention of leaving you two charming gentlemen alone, so we will all go together!"

This was Lord Mervyn's cue to collapse slowly and very convincingly from his chair onto the floor and even as he closed his eyes he heard Ali Pasha say to the Princess:

"You must have made it very strong!"

"The English, my dear Petrus," she replied in Turkish, "have not only an iron constitution, but also an iron stomach!"

"Then you must get him out of the way," he said. "But before you call the servants to carry him upstairs, let me commend you, Eudocia, and at the same time urge you to make quite certain that we learn something of importance. You know what I want to know."

"Yes, of course, dear Petrus, but go now. I do not know how long he will remain unconscious, and when he does awaken . . ."

She made a very eloquent and very French gesture with her hands and Ali Pasha laughed and said:

"He is a lucky man! I am only sorry I cannot take his place!"

"There will be other nights, dear Petrus," the Princess said softly, "which will be for pleasure, but tonight is dedicated to work."

Ali Pasha pulled the Princess against him and kissed her lips, then moved swiftly and silently from the room.

She waited until he was gone, then rang the small gold bell which stood on the table beside her place.

Two of her servants answered its summons and without waiting for orders picked up Lord Mervyn and carried him out of the room up the broad stairway to the next floor.

He kept his eyes closed and was apparently completely unconscious as they undressed him on a big soft bed with silk sheets that were scented with the same perfume that the Princess used on her body.

When they had left him he resisted an impulse to open his eyes and see where he was, knowing that while he might appear to be alone, there was more than likely somebody watching him of whom he was not aware.

Then softly, sinuously, the Princess came through a door which he heard open and close, and moved almost silently towards him.

Now he was aware that she was lying close beside him on the bed and he could feel the warmth of her body and the silken strands of her long dark hair touching his naked shoulder.

Slowly he turned his head from side to side and made an inarticulate murmur before he opened his eyes.

It was then the Princess moved closer to him and her hands were touching him, her voice, seductive and beguiling saying in his ear:

"*Mon Cher! Mon Brave!* We are alone, and what could be more entrancing?"

Lord Mervyn turned his head and looked at her in a manner which proclaimed it to be an effort for him to focus his eyes.

He saw then that he was lying in a bed draped with silk curtains in a room luxuriously furnished and filled with the fragrance of flowers.

As he was already aware, the Princess was close beside him and her body was against his, her lips lifted provocatively near to his mouth.

"What – has happened?" he asked in a slightly slurred voice.

"Does it matter?" the Princess asked. "We are together and, since I find you a very attractive man, let us forget everything but the pleasures of love and the inexpressible joy we can give each to each other."

She moved even closer to him as she spoke and Lord Mervyn said hazily:

"I – cannot remember what – happened after I – drank your – health."

"I can remember the very sweet things you said," the Princess replied, "and that is why it is a waste of time to talk when you might be kissing me."

As she spoke she moved nearer still and now her lips were against his and her arms were around his neck.

At that moment there was a loud knock on the door.

The Princess stiffened and raised her head.

The knock came again.

In an angry voice she enquired:

"What is it? I do not wish to be disturbed!"

"Your pardon, *Madame la Princesse*," a man's voice replied, "but somebody has called to see the gentleman who is with you on a matter of great urgency!"

"Called to see – me?" Lord Mervyn asked. "Who is it – and what has – happened?"

"The person says it's a matter of importance, M'Lord," the servant replied, "with instructions from the British Embassy that are awaiting Your Lordship at the hotel."

Lord Mervyn sat up in bed.

"Damn!" he swore fiercely. "Can I never have a moment to myself?"

"Do you have to leave me?" the Princess asked.

"What else can I do?" Lord Mervyn replied as if he were extremely irritated. "As you can quite understand, my dear, I would not wish it known either at our Embassy here or in London, that I was otherwise engaged when my presence was requested on an urgent matter."

"But what can be so urgent at this hour of the night?" the Princess asked.

Lord Mervyn got out of bed a little unsteadily and was relieved to see that his clothes had been placed on a chair on the other side of the room.

As he walked towards them he said:

"It is because of this cursed timing. In London they are still in their offices and doubtless the Foreign Office is working full blast!"

He put on his stiff white shirt and his slim black evening-trousers and shoes before he turned around to see the Princess lying back against the lace-trimmed pillows in her great bed looking extremely alluring and very seductive.

He was aware there was an expression of disappointment and frustration in her dark eyes.

As he adjusted his stiff collar and tied his tie, he walked towards her saying:

"How is it possible that a man can reach the gates of Heaven, only to be snatched away from them just as they were opening to him?"

The Princess smiled and threw out her hands.

"You express exactly my own feeling, *Mon Cher*. When will we see each other again?"

Lord Mervyn sat down on the bed facing her and said:

"You are very beautiful and I know any man would find you irresistible. At the same time, I also enjoy talking to you."

73

"As I want to talk to you," the Princess said. "Because it concerns you, I find myself, as I have never been before, very interested in India. Is it really true that the British are sending many more troops to protect themselves against the machinations of the Mad Fakir of whom Petrus was speaking at dinner?"

"I would not be surprised," Lord Mervyn replied vaguely, "but of course I was far too polite to your honoured guest to suggest that a great deal of encouragement has been given to the unrest on the North-West frontier by the Russians who have infiltrated Afghanistan."

He saw by the flicker in the Princess's eyes that she was aware of this and was surprised that he should know it too.

As if he was following his own train of thought Lord Mervyn said:

"Afghanistan is a country I have always wanted to visit. I wonder if Ali Pasha would be able to help me do so?"

"I am sure he would if I asked him," the Princess said. "After all, he knows the Amir well, and has many other contacts."

"Perhaps we could talk to him about it sometime."

"I will arrange another supper or dinner for the three of us," the Princess said, "and while we will of course talk politics, afterwards you and I could be alone, as we should have been alone now."

"Instead of which I have to leave you," Lord Mervyn said. "Could any man be more cruelly treated by fate?"

He rose from the bed as he spoke and walked across the room to put on his long-tailed evening-coat.

The Princess watched him, appreciating the broadness of his shoulders, the athletic slimness of his hips, and most of all his handsome face.

She knew that whatever she might have said to Ali Pasha about this being an evening for work, she had intended it

74

also to be an orgy of pleasure of which she was now being deprived.

With a little cry she sprang out of bed and ran towards Lord Mervyn flinging herself against him.

She was wearing a nightgown which was nothing more than a wisp of the finest chiffon trimmed with shadow lace.

Not only did it reveal every curve of her body, but as he put his arms around her he could feel vibrating from her the sensuous desire he had awakened.

With her arms around his neck and with her lips against his she whispered:

"Must you go? Do not leave me now. Send a message to say you are detained for at least an hour, perhaps two."

"I wish that were possible," Lord Mervyn replied, "but no one knows better than you that duty must come first."

He could not say any more because her lips, hungry, passionate and demanding, were on his.

Then as he released himself from her clinging arms she said:

"I will be in touch with you in the morning and, if you cannot dine tomorrow evening, it will be not later than the day after."

"I shall be waiting to hear from you," Lord Mervyn replied as he kissed her hand.

He walked towards the door and as he reached it he turned back to see her watching him, looking with her long dark hair falling over her naked shoulders so seductively desirable that it seemed strange that his eyes were hard as he walked down the stairs to where the servants were waiting at the front door.

As if he asked the question a senior servant bowed and said:

"The messenger, M'Lord, is waiting in the carriage outside."

"Thank you," Lord Mervyn replied.

He pressed the Turkish equivalent of a guinea into the servant's hand.

Then amid servile bows and salaams he walked down the steps and into the closed carriage.

The door was shut and as the horses drove off Lord Mervyn was aware that Rozella was sitting beside him, and he knew that Hunt would be on the box beside the coachman.

Rozella did not speak at once, and they had driven quite some way before she asked as if she could not control her curiosity:

"It was . . . all right? I had a little difficulty in . . . persuading the servants to . . . disturb you."

He did not answer, and after a moment she said:

"You were so long in coming I was . . . afraid that after all the drug had not been in the claret but in . . . something else and you had eaten or drunk it by mistake."

"You were quite right," Lord Mervyn said in a cold voice, "the claret was drugged, but I pretended to drink it."

Rozella gave a sigh of relief.

Then as she knew perceptively that because she was a woman he resented having to tell her anything about it, she lapsed into silence.

They drove without speaking until they reached the hotel and only when the carriage came to a standstill outside it did Lord Mervyn say:

"Thank you, Miss Beverly. You played your part most effectively."

"I am . . . glad."

He could not help knowing how anxious she had been.

"Please do not think I am impertinent," she added, "but I want to say how clever I thought it was of you that a message really did come from the Embassy about an hour ago."

Lord Mervyn turned his head to look at her for the first time.

Then he said with an air of surprise:

"Surely you are aware that in this country, as in any other, where everything one does is noted and scrutinised, one must never tell a lie one cannot substantiate."

It was something her father had said to her in the past which she had forgotten.

Now Rozella said humbly:

"Of course . . . it was stupid of me . . . to doubt for a moment that you would be so . . . efficient."

"You will find," Lord Mervyn said almost harshly, "that efficiency often means the difference between remaining alive or dying!"

With that he stepped out of the carriage, walked into the hall without looking back and went up the stairs to his own Suite.

Rozella was then helped out of the carriage by Hunt who had jumped down from the box-seat.

" 'All's well that ends well'!" he said with a grin. "His Lordship's home safe and sound, and we can all go to bed. If you're not tired, Miss, I am."

Rozella laughed.

There was something definitely warming about Hunt's cheery voice after the coldness and what she was sure was the disapproval of Lord Mervyn's.

She went upstairs to her room, pulled off the handkerchief which had covered her head, undressed and got into bed.

"At least I have proved myself useful today," she told herself before she went to sleep.

Then she knew nothing more until she was called, as she had asked to be, at eight o'clock the next morning.

Rozella breakfasted in her bedroom and as she waited for Lord Mervyn's summons she thought it was going to be very depressing if she was to have every meal alone and have no contact with him or anyone else unless she had an active job to do.

Then she told herself she was being very ungrateful.

She had travelled here in great comfort and had escaped through, she was certain, the mercy of God, from being sent back immediately as unsuitable.

Although it was too soon to expect to have anything of real importance to do, she was well aware that her part last night had been a vital one from Lord Mervyn's point of view.

She was not so stupid nor so innocent as not to realise what the Princess wanted of him, and she supposed that she must have interrupted them at a moment when, whether he was willing or not, the Princess was making love to him.

She was not quite certain what that entailed, but she thought if Lord Mervyn was in fact, as her mother had said, a misogynist, he would find it very difficult to play the part the Princess required.

Perhaps therefore her intervention with the story of an urgent message from the British Embassy had saved him from having to do something he disliked, or perhaps from failing to satisfy the demands of the Princess.

She could not quite reason it out for herself, but she was sure that something like that was entailed, and it was infuriating to think she would never know any more.

Instead she must remain for the rest of her life in ignorance as to what had actually occurred when she had forced by sheer willpower the servants to interrupt their mistress when they had been told explicitly not to do so.

"It is all very frustrating," she thought, "and yet in a way, exciting. I wonder what will happen next?"

She was so anxious that her heart seemed to leap excitedly when Hunt tapped on her door to tell her that Lord Mervyn was waiting to see her.

Once again when she entered his Suite it was to find him sitting at the desk.

When she had dropped him a polite curtsy and wished

him good-morning he said sharply:

"I cannot believe that your father revealed to you the Foreign Office code we use!"

"He spoke of it, My Lord," Rozella replied, "but he did not explain what it actually entailed. However I have an idea how codes work, and I do not think I would find it difficult to use one, should the occasion arise."

"Because it might be important in case of an accident," Lord Mervyn said, "I will show you what code we are using at the moment."

He again was speaking as if he was very reluctant to do so, but Rozella knew what he was really thinking was that if he were injured or killed, it would be important for her to be able to convey to the Foreign Office any information he had gathered but not yet imparted.

He indicated a chair beside his own at the desk, and as Rozella sat down he showed her the telegram he was sending in code and she saw with excitement that it was the information he had acquired last night.

He said that the man visiting the Princess was "NX3" and was in fact on friendly terms with Abdurrahman Khan the Amir of Afghanistan and a number of his Ministers.

He also said that he was quite convinced that the said "NX3" was aware that the Mad Fakir was working on instructions from the Russians in Afghanistan.

Rozella read the telegram quickly, then said:

"I have heard Papa speak of the Mad Fakir. Is he very dangerous?"

"Dangerous enough to be responsible for the loss of a large number of British lives," Lord Mervyn said sharply.

"Then the stories of the ambitions of the Russians in Afghanistan are true?"

As Rozella spoke she knew that Lord Mervyn was longing to tell her to mind her own business and not ask questions.

Then because he thought it was necessary for her to

know a little of what interested the Foreign Office, he said reluctantly:

"For the last two years, since 1893 when the Indo-Afghan frontier was demarcated, the British have been building up Afghanistan as a buffer State with gifts of arms and money."

Rozella was listening intently and he went on:

"At the same time, we are trying for the first time to subdue the tribes who have lived in semi-independence on the Indian side of the line. Roads are being built, boundary posts set up, forts established."

Lord Mervyn paused, then looked with unseeing eyes across the room, as if staring into the future as he said:

"Once content with controlling the plains at the foot of the mountains, we are now intent on holding the heads of all the passes, and this year Chitral, far to the north in the Hindu Kush, has been permanently garrisoned."

He was silent, and Rozella drew in her breath.

At last he was telling her the things she wanted to know; at last she was beginning to form a picture of why Lord Mervyn had wanted her father to come with him to Constantinople.

She knew, too, however much Lord Mervyn might dislike her personally, being with him on an adventure was different from anything she had imagined in her wildest fantasies.

It was very, very exciting.

Chapter Five

While having luncheon in her bedroom, which Rozella was beginning to find rather depressing, she was wondering whether it would be possible to ask Hunt to take her out into the City.

Although she felt it was something she should not do as her father's daughter, at the same time she was afraid that, unless she made a positive effort to see Constantinople, when she finally left she would only have seen the sights from her bedroom window apart from her brief visit with Hunt to the Spice Market.

"I suppose I could go alone?" she reasoned with herself.

She then had the feeling that it would not only be rather frightening, but at the same time something of which Lord Mervyn would disapprove.

While she was turning things over in her mind there was a knock on the door and Hunt came into the room.

"His Lordship's gone out for an hour," he announced, "but he's left you a cable to decode which is on his desk."

Rozella's eyes widened in surprise. This was something she had not expected, but, if Lord Mervyn trusted her, then that was certainly a step in the right direction.

"Come on, Miss," Hunt said, "I'll show you where the secret book's kept. If you loses it or somebody steals it, you'll either have your head chopped off, or else be shot at dawn!"

Rozella was laughing as he led the way to Lord Mervyn's Sitting-Room.

On the desk was an open telegram which obviously any spy could read without being excited about it.

It was in English and said:

MOTHER BETTER. DOCTOR DELIGHTED WITH
HER PROGRESS. HOPE TO HEAR FROM YOU
SOON.
LILIAN.

Hunt grinned as she finished reading it and said:

"Sounds nice and chatty, don't it, Miss? Now you'd better get down to work as His Lordship expects you to have everything done for his return."

As he spoke he walked across the room and picking up several rather heavy-looking books which were arranged near a side-table, he extracted one from the middle of the pile.

They were all in English, Rozella noticed, and she felt that anybody examining them would think that Lord Mervyn had an erudite, somewhat pedantic taste which the average reader would find unpalatable.

Hunt turned over several pages until he found the one he wanted, then he put the book down on the desk in front of Rozella.

She looked bewildered and Hunt laughed.

"This, Miss, is a real test of your ability!"

"What do I do?" Rozella asked.

"You see the name 'Lilian' at the bottom of the cable?" Hunt said. "Well, you counts each letter as a number of the alphabet, the first letter of Lilian being the twelfth. That means the sixth word in the twelfth line is the one you want, and the same applies to all the other letters of the name."

"It sounds very complicated," Rozella said.

"It has to be," Hunt replied. "Don't forget, Miss, them Orientals are expert at being mysterious and solving mysteries that the English find far too complex."

Rozella felt he was challenging her and she said:

"I will do my best, and I expect His Lordship has told you not to help me."

Hunt grinned.

"How did you guess?" he asked. "Well, good luck, Miss. And I wouldn't mind betting you'll confound His Lordship when he returns."

He went from the room as he spoke and Rozella sat down at the desk.

At first she thought her task was so complicated that she would be bound to make mistakes.

And yet, after half-an-hour, she had what appeared to be a perfectly sensible message which read:

BELIEVE AYUB LEFT PERSIA THREE DAYS AGO. CHECK IF POSSIBLE.

There was no signature, but it seemed to Rozella when she read it over that cryptic though the message might be, it should mean something dramatic to Lord Mervyn.

She was thinking of him when the door opened and he came in.

She rose to her feet and he asked:

"Have you finished?"

"I . . . I think so, My Lord!"

She thought, and it pleased her, that he was surprised when she held out her decoding of the cable.

He took it from her and she found herself praying that she had been clever enough to get it right if only to confound him.

He read slowly what she had written, then he said:

"I am astonished, Miss Beverly, although I suppose, since you are your father's daughter, I should not be, that you have managed to grasp this code so quickly. At the same time, it is quite a simple one."

"I guessed that, My Lord."

She spoke with a slight note of sarcasm in her voice and he looked at her quickly as if he thought she was mocking him.

Then he said in the sharp tone he had used to her before:

"Sit down. I have something to say to you!"

Apprehensively Rozella walked round the desk to sit on the hard seat which she had occupied the first day she had arrived.

Lord Mervyn sat down at the desk, pushed the telegram to one side and asked:

"You know what this means?"

"N-no, I do not think I do," Rozella replied.

Then the name 'Ayub' seemed somehow familiar and as she spoke she had the distinct feeling that Lord Mervyn was pleased by her ignorance.

She gave a little cry.

"I think I do know!" she exclaimed. "He is Ayub Khan who fled to Persia after he had been defeated at Kandahar!"

She knew as she spoke that Lord Mervyn was very surprised at what she had said, and she thought with a feeling of satisfaction that for the moment she had struck a blow at his complacency and what she had begun to think of as his almost detestable air of superiority.

There was a pause, then Lord Mervyn said as if the words were dragged from him:

"I congratulate you, Miss Beverly! You are, in fact, quite right. This cable does refer to Ayub Khan!"

Because she really wanted to know Rozella asked pleadingly:

"Will you please tell me more about him?"

"I wish I knew more," Lord Mervyn replied. "But you are quite right in remembering that he was defeated at Kandahar after the British had handed over to a governor deputed by the Amir Abdurrahman and had evacuated Afghanistan."

84

Rozella made a sound to show that she remembered this and Lord Mervyn went on:

"Ayub Khan had already been defeated in August 1880 by Lord Roberts with 10,000 picked soldiers, but after the departure of the British he once again seized Kandahar."

"He was then defeated," Rozella said quickly, "by the Amir who made him flee the country."

"Exactly!" Lord Mervyn agreed. "And since then Ayub Khan has been reported to be living in Persia."

Rozella thought for a moment. Then she said:

"Then why should he wish to come to Constantinople?"

"That is what we have to find out," Lord Mervyn said quietly, "and if he is here – who has invited him?"

Rozella felt her excitement growing.

"How can *we* discover that?" she asked.

She emphasised the word "we" feeling it was important that she should be included in what she felt already was going to be a desperate and perhaps dangerous involvement on the part of Lord Mervyn.

Then, as if the fact that she was excited annoyed him, Lord Mervyn brought his hand down sharply on the desk as he said:

"Make no mistake, Miss Beverly, I deeply regret and in fact, resent that you should be involved in an operation that should be essentially and entirely a masculine one."

For a moment Rozella felt that he was determined to cut her out if he could do so. Then she said quietly:

"At the same time if we find Ayub Khan and you cannot understand his speech, you will need me."

She saw from the way Lord Mervyn's eyes hardened and he pressed his lips together that she had hit the bull's-eye.

She knew the reason why he had needed her father so badly on this particular mission was that while her father spoke Pushtu and Persian fluently, Lord Mervyn probably had little more than a smattering of each language.

Pushtu was the mother tongue of the Pathans and most

common in East and South-East Afghanistan from Jala-labad to Kandahar.

"I can only take your word for it," Lord Mervyn said sourly, "that you will be able to understand as well as your father would what is said."

"I assure you I will not fail you," Rozella said confidently.

Lord Mervyn rose from the desk and walked across the room to stand at the window, and she had the idea that he was not seeing the sunshine on the roofs which also was turning the sea to gold.

Instead he was resenting with every fibre of his being that he was compelled against every inclination, to employ a woman.

She did not speak, she only sat looking at his back and thinking it was a pity that he, an attractive-looking man, should be so biased and, she told herself, so pig-headed.

It flashed through her mind that any ordinary man, although she had little knowledge of them, would have accepted the invitations of the seductive Princess Eudocia.

Yet Lord Mervyn had insisted upon being rescued quite unnecessarily early in the evening.

"It is stupid and wrong for a young man to cut himself off from what are the natural joys of life," she reasoned.

She was thinking of how happy her father and mother were together and how they would go upstairs with their arms entwined about each other, often forgetting to say 'goodnight' to her as she followed them.

Almost as if what she was thinking had communicated itself to him, Lord Mervyn turned round.

"You are right, Miss Beverly," he said briskly. "I should not think about you as a woman but convince myself that I have your father with me."

"I know my father would be very intrigued," Rozella said demurely.

"What I am trying to get into your head," he replied angrily, "is that this is an extremely dangerous operation, so dangerous in fact, that there is every likelihood of one or the other of us, perhaps both, dying before we can obtain the information that the Foreign Office requires."

The way he spoke made Rozella ask with a twinkle in her eyes which he could not see behind her tinted spectacles:

"Are you trying to frighten me, My Lord?"

"I am trying to make you understand," Lord Mervyn answered savagely, "that this is going to be no tea-party at the Vicarage, or fun and games like charades. This is serious, and the men we are investigating will stop at nothing to remain anonymous."

"I understand what you are saying to me," Rozella replied, "but I came here to take my father's place, and I hope that in whatever circumstances I find myself, I shall behave with the same courage and the same intelligence as he would."

The quiet manner in which she spoke obviously impressed Lord Mervyn, for after a moment he said:

"Very well, and although it is against my better judgement, there is apparently nothing I can do about it."

Then curtly, almost as if he was ordering her like a raw recruit to obey him, he said:

"Be ready to leave in half-an-hour, and I warn you we may not be able to return, if we *do* return, until after midnight."

He walked as he spoke through the communicating door which led to his bedroom.

As he shut it somewhat forcefully behind him Rozella stared after him in surprise.

It seemed to her he was behaving very differently from the way she might have expected and there was in fact, an element of emotion in his aggressive attitude.

Then she asked herself what did it matter as long as she

87

was not left alone to wonder what he was doing and feel she had been shut out of all the action, whatever that might entail.

Hurriedly she went to her bedroom to take from her head the silk handkerchief with which she had covered her hair, and instead to pin it up so that she could put on her father's ugly mackintosh hat in its place.

It was warm outside and she had therefore worn a light summer gown and covered it with Nanny's woollen shawl.

She decided however that as they were going to stay out late, it would be best, even though it was hot, to wear either the coat in which she had travelled, or else her father's long woollen jacket which in the heat of the afternoon would be too warm.

She had little choice and decided to wear the woollen jacket. Looking in the glass she thought she looked so ugly that she would not be surprised if Lord Mervyn refused to take her with him.

Then she remembered with a leap of her heart that however much he might resent it, she was indispensable.

Although they might not find, as he hoped, Ayub Khan, at least she would be with him and perhaps would impress him with her intelligence.

At the same time it was a pity they could not be more friendly.

She wondered why, out of all the men in the world, with whom her father might have co-operated, he had chosen a misogynist who obviously would hate her, whatever she looked like, and whatever age she might be.

She began telling herself a fairy-story in which Lord Mervyn was quite different from what he actually was, and there was no need for her to be disguised or pretend to be anything but a pretty young girl.

They would laugh together and talk over what lay ahead and plan the destruction of the enemy.

Because Rozella, being an only child, had been alone so much, the stories she told herself were to her very real.

She could think herself into being a part of them until the ordinary, everyday world vanished and she was living in a Fairyland where everything worked out just as she wanted it to.

She was in fact, imagining herself dressed in a new and expensive gown which the Lord Mervyn of her dreams had considered it important for her to wear so that she could entice and perhaps even seduce the enemy when a knock at the door brought her sharply back to reality.

She realised it would probably be Lord Mervyn who now wanted her, and she quickly walked across the room to open the door.

As she anticipated, he was waiting outside and he asked:

"Are you ready?"

"Yes, My Lord."

She thought he deliberately looked away from her as if the sight of her repelled him.

"The carriage is waiting," he said, "and we are leaving by a side-door."

He walked away down the passage obviously determined she should ask no questions, and as she followed him she kept a pace or so behind in case he thought she was intruding.

The carriage waiting at the side-door was the ordinary open kind of vehicle that could be hired in any street of Constantinople. The only difference was that Hunt was sitting on the box beside the coachman.

A servant from the hotel closed the carriage-door after they had stepped into it and they drove off.

Once again Rozella was fascinated by the crowds in the streets, and as she was certain Lord Mervyn did not wish to talk to her, she amused herself by trying to guess from what part of Turkey they came. She also saw a number of men

89

who obviously came from other countries.

The carriage stopped when they reached the outside of the covered Bazaar.

Lord Mervyn got out, and as Rozella joined him he started to walk in a bored manner amongst the people staring into the small shops on either side of the covered way.

They were haggling with the sellers of fruit and sweet-meats or wandering down the centre of the great Bazaar, as if bemused by other passers-by who were doing the same thing.

Lord Mervyn did not speak, but occasionally he stopped outside a shop with its windows filled with jewels and attractive objects in gold and silver.

Rozella would have liked to go inside and look more closely at the jewellery that she suspected was cheap by English standards. For she knew that many of the pieces were made by craftsmen whose skill had been passed down for many centuries.

But they passed on after an inspection of only a few moments, and Lord Mervyn appeared to be aimlessly wandering and to anybody watching was just another tourist.

Rozella however knew he was moving steadily towards some objective, although she had no idea what it could be.

She was aware that Hunt was not far behind them, eating some strange fruit which he had bought from one of the stalls, and occasionally exchanging a friendly word with some child who bumped into him or with a vendor whose goods he did not require.

Suddenly, so quickly that Lord Mervyn took Rozella by surprise, he caught hold of her arm and pulled her through a doorway that she had not even been aware was there until she had passed through it.

Hunt came in behind them, then closed the door, and she heard a key turn in the lock.

Then they were moving down a dark passage until, as is

common in Turkey, they came to a small court-yard with a well in the centre of it.

A man appeared who salaamed to Lord Mervyn, and led the way across the court-yard into another passage as narrow and dark as the one they had just left.

He opened a door, and when they had all three passed into the room inside, the door was closed behind them.

Suddenly Lord Mervyn's detached, contemptuous air changed and he said sharply to Rozella:

"Change behind that curtain into the *burnous* you will find there. Take off your stockings, and Hunt will tint your face and hands with henna."

As he spoke he pulled aside the curtain that covered part of the room, and as Rozella went behind it, the curtain fell back into place.

She could hear the two men in the other room removing their shoes, and she thought, their clothes.

Thrown over a chair there was a black *burnous* of the type worn by every Muslim woman, and on the floor a pair of the flat sandals with a leather sole held in place only by a strap which she knew was extremely uncomfortable.

There was however no time to think, and quickly she took off her jacket, glad that she was wearing a thin gown underneath it.

Only as she lifted off her hat did she realise with dismay that she had no silk handkerchief with which to conceal her hair.

She told herself however that covered by the *burnous* which was the most concealing garment in the world it would not matter to Lord Mervyn or anybody else whether she was bald or grey-headed.

She therefore pressed firmly into place the pins with which she held her hair on top of her head, before covering it with the hat.

As she put on the *burnous* she realised that there was a *yashmak* which she could wear instead of her spectacles.

This concealed her eyes and she thought it unlikely that anyone would look at her closely enough to realise they were not as dark as they should be.

They were actually green flecked with gold and, as her father had said once, reminded him of a clear mountain stream.

"I will keep my eyes half-closed," Rozella told herself.

She also pulled her *burnous* well over her forehead and thought it would be impossible for even her mother and father to recognise her.

It was then from on the other side of the curtains that Hunt spoke for the first time, and he asked:

"Can I come in, Miss?"

"Yes, I am ready," Rozella replied, pulling off her last stocking as she spoke and placing it on the chair with her gown and her jacket.

Hunt came through the curtain and she saw that he carried in his hand a saucer containing the henna with which every Eastern woman darkened her nails, the palms of her hands, and the soles of her feet.

He treated Rozella's hands first, and she thought because her nails were long the henna made them look very attractive.

He then painted the soles of her feet, and she slipped on the uncomfortable flat sandals, hoping she would not have to walk far.

When Hunt had finished, Rozella went through the curtains to stand still for a moment, astonished when she saw Lord Mervyn. Thinking only of her own disguise, she had not considered what his would be.

Now she saw in front of her a Turkish man wearing a red *fez*, the shapeless trousers that were tight around the ankle, and over them, as so many Turks assumed in the colder months of the year, a badly cut and badly fitting Western jacket.

That was strange enough, but he was also wearing small

and extremely ugly steel-rimmed spectacles, and she was aware that his skin had been darkened until he looked very different from the aristocratic English gentleman with whom she had left the hotel.

She thought he inspected what he could see of her critically and then he said to Hunt:

"You know where to meet us?"

"I'll be there, M'Lord," Hunt replied, "and good luck!"

As he spoke to his master he looked at Rozella who smiled at him behind her *yashmak*.

Then shuffling uncomfortably in her sandals she followed Lord Mervyn as he went ahead.

They did not go back to the Bazaar, but went instead through a door at the end of the passage. This led them out into a dirty yard piled with sacks and boxes that obviously belonged to one of the shops.

From this there was an outer door that led into a lane of rough cobble-stones and after passing several buildings led onto a wider road in which was waiting an open carriage.

It was like the one in which they had left the hotel, drawn by a tired, underfed horse, and driven by an elderly man with a long beard.

He made no attempt to descend and open the door for them, and once they were in the carriage set off without speaking, bringing his whip down hard on the back of his ancient horse that made no effort to go any faster.

Slowly, moving laboriously along the twisting streets in which there were a few Muslim women dressed like Rozella, they came to a part of the City where the houses were very poor, many of them so dilapidated that they were empty and deserted.

They drove on until in front of them were the ruins of what had once been a large and important mosque.

Several of the minarets had long since lost their pointed tops, while the domes, and there were a number of them, had gaping holes in their green roofs.

Vegetation had grown over what was left of the lower walls of the building until in some places they were completely covered by it.

The carriage came to a standstill and Lord Mervyn paid the driver. Without a word of thanks he merely whipped up his horse and drove away.

Rozella waited, wondering what was to happen next.

Lord Mervyn walked in front of her as any Eastern man would have done, and she followed him shuffling over the broken paving-stones and dusty ground until they came to where in front of them there was a large hole in the wall.

Here Lord Mervyn paused.

He turned then as if to look at Rozella behind him, but she was aware his eyes were searching further afield as if he were afraid they were being followed.

Reassured he turned, and moving swiftly he bent his head and went through the gaping hole in the wall which had once been part of the main hall of the mosque.

Inside vegetation blocked what had once been windows and Lord Mervyn walked on until he came to a small twisting stone staircase.

Here also, creeping ivy had covered the first two steps, and Lord Mervyn climbed over it carefully so as not to crush the leaves, and perceptively Rozella knew that this was what she must do too.

Then they were climbing, twisting in a spiral round what she knew must once have been one of the smaller domes of the mosque.

She was, in fact, not surprised when after they had climbed for perhaps twenty feet she found herself entering a dome.

It was high enough for them to walk across it with their backs bent, and when they sat they could sit upright without the roof even touching Lord Mervyn's head.

He sat, to Rozella's surprise, Eastern fashion, with his legs bent under him, and because it was something she had learned to do as a child, she followed his example, pulling her *burnous* round her.

Then for the first time Lord Mervyn spoke in a very low voice and in Turkish.

"If we are discovered," he said, "which is unlikely, we are two lovers who come here because we have been forbidden to meet by our parents."

"Otherwise, what are we waiting for?" Rozella asked.

In reply Lord Mervyn moved his hand about a foot in front of him and very gently lifted up several broken pieces of plaster with which the floor was covered.

Looking straight down Rozella could see a room beneath them.

It was a round and comparatively small one, but large enough to hold perhaps a dozen or more people.

Rozella also noticed that on the floor there were a number of cushions, shabby and rather faded, on which the Muslim priests had once sat when they read from the *Koran*.

"I am afraid we may have a long wait," Lord Mervyn said. "In fact, I may have been misinformed, and it is not tonight that they are meeting here."

"And who are 'they'?" Rozella asked.

She felt as she asked the question that Lord Mervyn resented it because he himself was not certain, but after a moment's pause he replied:

"I am informed on good authority that it is here that the heads of the Young Ottomans meet when they are plotting how to bring about the downfall of the Sultan."

"And you think they are involved with the man who interests London?"

She did not say his name, thinking it might be indiscreet since even in this deserted mosque the walls might have ears.

As if Lord Mervyn appreciated her caution he replied:

"We are working in the dark, and we can only wait to

see, and pray if you say your prayers, that we shall not be discovered."

There was no need for him to tell her that if anyone discovered them, whether Young Ottomans, or those who were interested in other countries further afield, they would resent being spied upon.

Rozella realised with a shiver that they would then take the necessary precautions to ensure that whatever had been overheard could not be repeated.

Despite her resolution not to show Lord Mervyn she was afraid, she shivered and he said:

"Your father and I have been in worse situations, and our luck has never failed us."

Carefully he put back the pieces of plaster he had removed, and Rozella guessed that he was taking every precaution in case the first-comers should look around and suspect that they were being watched or overheard.

After that they sat in silence, but Rozella felt Lord Mervyn's vibrations emanating from him, and in a strange way it was as if he were talking to her.

She was aware that he was straining every nerve in order to acquire for England the information that was so vitally needed by the Foreign Office.

It made him seem more human and she found herself praying that he would be successful.

Rozella understood that Britain was determined to keep the balance of power not only in the Far East, but also in the countries nearer home.

She found herself thinking how in the last year Turkey had lost so much respect by encouraging the persecution of the Armenians by the Kurds.

Her father was also sure that sooner or later Turkey would go to war with Greece over Crete, while the British and the other great powers did not want a conflict in the Mediterranean.

She had the feeling that Lord Mervyn was thinking just

the same as she was, and she wondered how it was possible that she could feel, because they were sitting silent and close to each other, that she was more attuned to him than she had been since her arrival.

She thought she hated him, and yet she knew it was impossible to hate any man who was willing to take such risks as were in his position quite unnecessary.

At home he had his estates, his position in the House of Lords, his horses, and a dozen other interests.

And yet he was prepared to risk his life to help British Diplomacy keep the wild men of other countries under control.

She could understand the frustrations of the Young Ottomans when progress under the present Sultan had come to a complete stop.

But secret societies and revolutionary acts which invariably began and ended with killing, were not the right way to change his policy.

Rozella was trying to recall in her mind everything her father had said in the past and wishing she could remember more, when there was a faint movement beneath them and she felt Lord Mervyn stiffen.

Then there was the sound of footsteps, not very loud, since because the mosque had once been sacred whoever it was would have removed his shoes.

A second later voices, low and speaking in Turkish, could be heard, and there was a sound as if two men were moving the cushions. Then there was clearly the voice of another arrival.

As he spoke in more or less a normal tone, as if he was completely confident of not being overheard, Lord Mervyn made a slight movement, and Rozella knew that he had recognised the voice.

She suspected, almost as if she was reading his thoughts, that the man who had now entered the room beneath them was the man he had met last night with the Princess.

She did not know how she knew this, but at times in the past she had had presentiments that proved to be true, and she was sure this was another of them.

Now there were sounds of other arrivals, and very gently Lord Mervyn began to remove the pieces of broken plaster that he had replaced in the hole in the floor.

It was quite a small hole, and Rozella guessed that the ceiling beneath them was dark and dirty with age. Since she and Lord Mervyn were sitting in darkness it would be impossible, or almost impossible, for anyone below to notice the small hole through which they could see quite clearly the people below them.

She bent her head and saw that lanterns were being lit below them which hung from hooks on the wall.

Now she could see quite clearly a good-looking man seated directly below them, while two other men had moved into the background to sit on the floor, obviously not being of enough importance to command a cushion.

There were two other men there, both she was sure, of some distinction judging by the way they were greeted by the first.

Then there was a sound outside the room and a moment later a man came in.

By the light from the lanterns Rozella could see he had high cheekbones and a harsh, cruel face which was markedly different from that of the Turks who were greeting him.

Distinctly she heard the newcomer say:

"Ali Pasha! This is a great day when we meet again because I know you will help me!"

There was a little pause, before Ali Pasha replied:

"Ayub Khan – I and everything I possess are yours!"

Rozella gave a little gasp.

Now she knew that Lord Mervyn had been right and the man he had been waiting for was there.

Without thinking she put out her hand, and as if he

98

understood her excitement and wished to quell it, his fingers closed firmly over hers.

Below them Ayub Khan sat down on a cushion next to Ali Pasha and started to talk in Pushtu, the language of the Pathans, which Rozella had expected him to use.

As he spoke she was thankful that it was a language she knew well, and in which she and her father had often conversed together.

Still holding onto Lord Mervyn's hand she was listening intently – listening to a man whose hatred of the British seemed to vibrate round the room beneath them and to rise like an evil genie up towards them, menacing, violent and treacherous.

It was so frightening that involuntarily Rozella's fingers tightened on Lord Mervyn's.

As she listened she knew that whatever the risk to themselves, they must somehow prevent this fanatic, this fiend who was already responsible for the deaths of many British soldiers, from attaining power.

The two men talked, plotted and planned while those around them listened in silence, although Rozella was sure that with the exception of Ali Pasha they did not understand Pushtu.

Occasionally Ali Pasha would break in to translate what Ayub Khan had said, when the others would bend forward, afraid to miss a word, and the tension seemed to grow.

It was clear to Rozella what Ayub Khan intended, the first phase being to murder the Amir Abdurrahman and take over Afghanistan.

After that he would annihilate the British on the North-West Frontier and gradually percolate with all the troops he could muster down into India.

It was a grandiose scheme, a frightening one, but Rozella knew that Ayub Khan was absolutely convinced that it was practicable and he would soon reign supreme in Afghanistan, as he had always intended to do.

Then she heard Ali Pasha promise that he would provide Ayub Khan with the weapons he required – modern weapons, weapons even better than those possessed by the British.

"Turks will give you some now," he said. "The rest are waiting for you . . ."

"In Russia!" Ayub Khan added with relish.

"Exactly!" Ali Pasha agreed. "I have spoken about you, and the Russians are whole-heartedly on your side against the British they loathe and detest! The more British that are killed, the better they will be pleased!"

"Then we must please them!" Ayub Khan said.

Rozella listening could visualise his eyes glistening evilly in the light from the lanterns.

They drank a toast to the future and those present who were Rozella guessed the leaders of the Young Ottomans, pledged themselves to assist in every way possible.

They then assured Ayub Khan that their followers amongst the students in the military and medical schools were very numerous.

They were all, Rozella learned, being disciplined and trained in readiness for the revolt against the Sultan.

Now as they gave Ayub Khan their names, they promised to lay their lives at his feet.

There was Talat Bey who said he was the Chief Clerk of the Salonika Post Office and a student of law, and Rahmi Bey, who had formed a secret society of Union and Progress to restore the constitution.

They were talking Turkish, so now Lord Mervyn also could understand what they were saying.

At the same time, Rozella forced herself to memorise every name, everything they said, so that if they got away without being discovered, it could be reported in every detail to London.

Finally after what seemed a long time Ayub Khan rose to his feet.

He was going back, he said, to the place where he was hiding, but he would be in touch with his friends, and the next step was for Ali Pasha to tell the Russians what was intended.

After many good-byes and Eastern expressions of devotion, Ayub Khan left with the two men who had come with him and who had never spoken a word from the moment they arrived.

As soon as they had gone those who were left behind did not begin to talk amongst themselves, as Rozella had expected they would.

Instead, taking the lanterns from the walls they followed Ali Pasha who moved swiftly away, and their silence seemed more ominous than if they had chatted or even cheered as young Englishmen in the same circumstances might have done.

With Oriental secrecy, softness of foot, and in utter silence they left the room.

Only as the lights went with them did Rozella with a little sigh realise that she and Lord Mervyn were now sitting in the dark and still holding hands.

She would have taken her hand from his, but he held it for a moment, and she could feel his excitement emanating electrically from him like a Life Force pouring towards her.

Because he did not move she did not move either.

Then after what seemed a long time he released her hand and rose from his sitting position to move across to the opening that led to the staircase.

Rozella followed him, aware that her knees were aching after being in the same position for so long.

She felt, however, that nothing mattered except that they had achieved what they had set out to do. Not only did she feel as elated as Lord Mervyn, but she knew she had a great deal to tell him which she was sure he had not understood.

Very slowly and quietly they descended the twisting

staircase and she knew he was taking every precaution in case somebody had been left behind on watch who would report that they were there.

In which case the secret of what they had seen and heard would die with them.

Outside night had fallen, the stars were bright in the sky and a young moon was pouring its pale light over the ruined mosque.

Lord Mervyn moved quickly over the rough pavement and past the ruined walls until they came to the entrance by which they had come in.

To Rozella's relief there was a closed carriage waiting for them there, and she saw it was driven by Hunt.

He watched their approach, but made no movement to relinquish the reins.

Lord Mervyn opened the door and helped Rozella into the carriage, and as he jumped in beside her, Hunt moved off.

They all knew it was imperative that they should get back to the hotel safely, and without anybody being aware of where they had been.

For a moment she felt quite limp at the relief and also exhausted from the tension in which, without realising it, she had listened with every nerve and muscle alert in her body.

Then as the horses Hunt was driving gathered speed, Lord Mervyn said in an ordinary, quiet voice:

"Your clothes are on the seat in front of you, Miss Beverly. It may be rather uncomfortable, but we have to change back into being ourselves before we reach the hotel."

Chapter Six

Rozella with a sense of relief pulled the *burnous* off her head and slipped it down onto the floor.

Then she remembered the *yashmak* which, although in the excitement of the moment she had not been aware of it, had been hurting the bridge of her nose.

She realised that beside her in the darkness Lord Mervyn was starting to undress, and she reached forward onto the small seat in front to find her stockings.

They were lying on top of her jacket and her hat and she put them on, having the idea that she was being rather clumsy while Lord Mervyn from long practice was, though with far more undressing to do, being neater and swifter than she was.

Having fastened her stockings and pulled down her gown she groped forward to find her shoes.

As she did so, unexpectedly the carriage came to a stop and Rozella raised her head to see what was happening.

Then she heard wailing voices and she was aware that they were waiting for a funeral to pass, the dead body being held high in the centre of the road and followed by a large number of mourners all of whom were wailing noisily.

Rozella was so interested that she peered intently at what was happening and found she could see quite clearly because a number of the men walking beside the mourners were carrying flaring torches.

Then as the light from a passing torch flooded into the interior of the carriage she was aware that Lord Mervyn was sitting back on the seat looking at her.

She could see him quite clearly, his eyes staring at her.

Then as she looked at him suddenly she was conscious that her hair which had come unpinned under the *burnous* was falling untidily over her shoulders, while her eyes, looking back at him, were no longer concealed by her tinted spectacles.

With a little exclamation of horror she turned her head away, but as she did so the funeral procession passed on, the torch-bearers with them, and Hunt started forward again.

Rozella felt her heart beating uncomfortably, but she did not speak.

Picking up her hat she pressed her untidy hair into it and put her spectacles back onto her nose.

Then she found her shoes and her jacket, and only when she was fully dressed did she find that Lord Mervyn had been far quicker than she had been and sitting motionless beside her was, she was sure, extremely annoyed.

He did not speak, and since her heart was pounding heavily in her breast and she thought her voice had died in her throat, she too sat in silence.

At the same time, she was vividly aware that there were a thousand questions unanswered between them.

As they drove on Rozella tried to think of some plausible explanation she could offer but it was difficult to put into words what she was feeling.

All she could wonder was if he was furiously angry at being deceived, or whether if he thought it over quietly he would decide she had been sensible, if she had to travel alone to Constantinople, to have adopted a guise which was as protective as any chaperon could be.

Knowing Lord Mervyn's feelings about women, she felt she could reassure him that looking as she did she was in no way a menace to him as a man.

Although in her mind she was sure she had done the right thing, she was afraid she would never find the words to convince him that it was so.

It was too dark for her to see him, but once again she could feel his vibrations pulsating towards her, and she was sure he was angry, in fact, so angry that he would probably send her away on the first train out of Constantinople.

Then she remembered with a leap of her heart that he did not know exactly what Ayub Khan and Ali Pasha had said to each other in Pushtu.

However furious he might be with her as an individual, what mattered to him most at the moment was to learn from her the vital information that was hers and hers alone and convey it to London.

By the time they reached the hotel and Hunt had drawn the carriage to a standstill outside the side-door, Rozella was reassuring herself that, because she was still of some use to Lord Mervyn, he would not dare to condemn her as violently as he might otherwise have done.

At the same time, she thought despairingly that he would certainly make things more difficult than they were already, and perhaps, however much he needed her to fill her father's place, he would send her home.

She knew that to have to return after so short a time in Constantinople would be a bitter blow, and she had a sudden impulse to beg him to give her another chance.

But this was impossible because Lord Mervyn was already bending forward to open the carriage-door, and when he had done so and stepped out there was nothing Rozella could do but follow him.

Without asking any question she left her burnous and yashmak and the sandals she had worn on the seat where she had put them, knowing that Hunt, when he had disposed of the carriage, would deal with anything left inside it.

Without waiting for her Lord Mervyn walked ahead up the side staircase which led to their rooms, and as he reached his Sitting-Room he opened the door, then waited for Rozella to precede him into it.

"... I would like to ... tidy myself ... My Lord," she said in a low voice.

"Very well, but be quick!" he replied.

Alarmed by the way he spoke, she ran the short distance down the corridor to her bedroom, went in, and looking at her reflection in the mirror was horrified at what she saw.

Her hat was pressed over her eyes at an angle, the henna on her hands had stained her face also and she thought too there was an accumulation of dust on her skin.

Quickly she pulled off her hat and washed her face and hands in the basin. Then she covered her hair with the silk handkerchief she had used before.

She had removed her jacket as she entered the room and picked up Nanny's grey shawl from where she had left it on a chair and put it round her shoulders.

As she adjusted her spectacles she thought she now looked again exactly as Lord Mervyn had seen her ever since she had arrived and she hoped that he would dismiss the brief glimpse he had had of her in the carriage as an illusion and would not refer to it.

Because she was aware that he was waiting impatiently concerned with what he had not been able to understand when the two men had talked in Pushtu, she hurried back to the Sitting-Room.

She opened the door and went in to find Lord Mervyn as she had expected, sitting at his desk with the book that contained the code open in front of him.

She sat down in the upright chair opposite him and waited for him to begin asking the questions to which she was sure he was impatient to know the answers.

He raised his head, put down the pen he held in his hand, then said:

"Take that ridiculous handkerchief off your head and remove those hideous spectacles! There is no reason for you to continue trying to deceive me!"

It was not what Rozella had expected him to say and for a moment she did not move.

Then she said:

"I . . . I am sorry if I have deceived you . . . but I thought it the . . . best thing to do."

"If you mean that you deceived me into thinking you were a middle-aged woman, you are very much mistaken!"

What he said now was even more unexpected and Rozella stared at him almost open-mouthed.

"Y-you . . . knew?"

"Of course I knew that you were not what you pretended to be," he answered. "I am not entirely half-witted! And as I happened to remember the year that your father was married, I knew it would be impossible for you to be anything but a girl of nineteen."

Rozella blushed.

She felt humiliated that he should think her so stupid, and she was sure he was speaking contemptuously.

She did not argue with him further but took off her spectacles and undid the silk handkerchief she had tied pirate-fashion at the base of her neck.

What she had forgotten was that in her hurry she had not pinned her hair securely in place as she usually did, and now it fell onto her shoulders.

The light from the oil-lamp on the table picked out the red lights in it, making it seem to dance over her head like little flames.

She was aware that Lord Mervyn was staring at her with what she thought was a hostile expression and she looked at him pleadingly.

Because she was afraid her eyes seemed to fill her whole face.

Then curtly he said:

"Now let us get down to business! Tell me exactly what Ayub Khan said to Ali Pasha."

"You do not understand Pushtu?" Rozella asked.

"Not enough to follow a long conversation in detail," Lord Mervyn admitted.

"Then I will tell you exactly what they said."

She clasped her fingers together in her lap and like a child reciting a lesson went back to the beginning when Ayub Khan arrived in the room below them.

She recited almost word for word everything that had been said until they departed.

She knew as she spoke that her memory was phenomenal thanks to her father who had taught her ever since she was a small child, to learn quickly, until by the time she was ten she could read a poem and recite it accurately a few minutes later.

Now she thought with a feeling of satisfaction that however angry Lord Mervyn might be with her for other reasons, he could not fault the manner in which she had carried out her task in unmasking Ayub Khan's treachery.

As she spoke he was making notes rapidly, and she was sure competently, in a notebook in front of him.

When she had finished speaking he looked down at what he had written and drew in his breath as if he could hardly believe it was true.

Then he said:

"I never expected – I never imagined that Ayub Khan would attempt anything on such a grandiose scale or that Ali Pasha would be so deeply involved."

He spoke as if he was talking to himself. Then as he remembered that Rozella was there he said:

"You have nothing else to add to what you have just told me?"

"I am sure I have remembered everything, My Lord."

"Then I suggest you go to bed."

"You do not need me to help in translating it into code?"

"No, I will do it myself."

Then he hesitated and, as Rozella was wondering what

he was thinking, he rose to his feet.

"Wait here!" he said abruptly and walked from the room.

She looked after him in bewilderment, thinking he was behaving strangely and making himself even more difficult to understand than usual.

Then because she felt embarrassed she twisted her hair at the back of her head and found two hairpins to hold it in place.

Lord Mervyn was away for so long that Rozella began to think he must have forgotten about her.

Then as she was wondering what had happened he came back into the room, and before he shut the door she had a glimpse of Hunt behind him in the corridor.

Lord Mervyn walked to his desk.

"Hunt thinks that we left unobserved," he said quietly, "and there is no reason why anybody should suspect we were anywhere tonight but with friends and in another part of the City."

Rozella was listening, wondering why he had been so anxious.

"There is however no point in taking chances," he went on. "I therefore do not intend to send the cable with the information we have just acquired until we are outside the country."

"Outside : . . Turkey?" Rozella asked, trying to understand.

"We will leave tomorrow on the Orient Express," Lord Mervyn said. "Meanwhile your room has been changed. 'Miss Beverly' checked out earlier this evening, and a relative of mine, a Mrs Lynne, has just checked in."

"I . . . I do not understand."

"You will see it more clearly in the morning," Lord Mervyn said. "Now go to bed. Hunt is waiting outside to show you your new room, and I am sure you will sleep well."

As he spoke he opened the communicating door which led into his bedroom and left without saying any more.

Rozella stared after him in astonishment.

It seemed incredible after all they had been through together that he did not want to talk about it, and she did not understand why she should change her identity.

There was however nothing else she could do but go into the corridor to find Hunt, who was waiting for her, grinning cheerily as he went ahead of her past her previous bedroom to open another door a little further away.

It was a large, comfortable room very like the one she had been sleeping in before, and she saw that Hunt had brought in her nightgown which she suspected the chambermaid had laid out ready on her bed, but nothing else.

She looked at him for explanation and he shut the door into the corridor before he said:

"His Lordship's taking no chances, Miss, and if you asks me, that's sensible of him!"

"I do not understand," Rozella said as she had said to his master.

"Well, it's like this," Hunt said in a low tone. "You've caused quite a lot of comment, looking like you do and being in His Lordship's *entourage* so to speak. So now you've gone and they won't hear any more about you."

"But . . . but my clothes!" Rozella exclaimed.

"I'll dispose of them, Miss," Hunt said, "including that ugly hat and that coat you arrived in."

"But . . . what am I to wear?" Rozella asked weakly.

She had the feeling that she should resent Hunt talking in such a familiar way, and yet, perhaps because she was tired after all the excitement, she felt as if she could not grasp what the arrangements were.

Even if she objected, she felt she was far too feeble to do anything about it.

"Now you go to sleep, Miss, and leave everything to His

110

Lordship," Hunt said. "He's got it all planned out, and once we're all on the Orient Express we'll feel a sight better than we do now."

"Are you . . . implying that we are . . . still in . . . danger?" Rozella asked in a frightened little voice.

"Of course we are in danger!" Hunt replied. "It only wants one 'Nosey Parker' seein' you and His Lordship coming out of the ruins, and the carriage waiting at a time of night when there's few people about, for somebody to 'put two and two together'!"

"I thought you told His Lordship that we were not fol- lowed," Rozella persisted.

"How can I or anyone else be certain of that?" Hunt asked. "But as long as its 'okey-dokey' tomorrow night we can tell a very different story, and His Lordship's bein' very protective where you're concerned."

"Why me in particular?" Rozella queried.

Hunt shrugged his shoulders.

"Search me," he replied. "All I can say, Miss, is, looking as you do now, it would be a pity to have what they calls 'an unfortunate accident'."

He grinned at her, then he said:

"It'll all come clear tomorrow morning, but remember you knows nothing about Miss Beverly who left the hotel early this evening before the night staff came on duty, and if anyone asks me I'll say: 'I thinks she's gone sight-seein', perhaps to Ephesus.' "

There was a hint of laughter in Hunt's voice, then he left the room shutting the door quietly behind him.

Rozella sat down on the bed.

She could hardly believe what she had just heard, and that Lord Mervyn had suddenly given her a new identity.

Then unexpectedly she found herself laughing.

It was all so fantastic, and yet in a way exactly what she might have expected if she was taking the place of her father.

As she undressed and got into bed, she was thinking of how Lord Mervyn had said she had not deceived him; that he had known all along that she was a young girl.

That somehow made it embarrassing, although she could not explain why, except that it was humiliating to think that he had been aware she was disguised and, she was quite certain, had not been impressed by her amateurish efforts.

Perhaps he had been laughing at her, but more probably he had felt scornful and contemptuous that she was not more effective.

She could not help realising that when he had disguised himself as a Turk it would have been almost impossible for anybody to suspect that he was anything else.

'He must think me very foolish not to have guessed that if I said I was my father's daughter he would somehow check on my age,' Rozella reasoned.

She wished now she had said she was her father's sister. That would have been far more suitable for her disguise and more likely to have persuaded Lord Mervyn to accept her, believing she had been sent to him by the man he admired and with whom he had worked before.

'It is a good thing Lord Mervyn is not one of the enemy,' Rozella thought, 'or I should be dead by now for making such a stupid mistake!'

As she drifted off to sleep she found herself thinking that Lord Mervyn had never praised her for her skill in remembering the conversation between Ayub Khan and Ali Pasha so accurately.

He had in fact been so abrupt that she could only think that he now disliked her even more than he had before, and once they had left Turkey would make sure he had nothing to do with her ever again.

She wondered why the idea was so depressing, and also why she would have liked him, however much he disapproved of her as a woman, to say she had played her part well, and had at least obtained the information he needed just as intelligently as her father would have done.

"I have done my best," she said wistfully into the darkness.

Then, probably because she was so very tired, she felt the tears come into her eyes and knew quite unaccountably they were tears of disappointment.

Rozella slept until quite late in the morning. In fact, it was ten o'clock when there was a knock on her door and she roused herself to say: "Come in!"

It was her breakfast, and being in fact, very hungry she ate with relish.

Only after she had finished her second cup of coffee did she look at the clock and exclaim in horror that it was so late.

There was however no sign of anyone to rebuke her, and she thought, although she was not sure, that the Orient Express left Constantinople for Paris in the afternoon.

She was just considering whether she should get up when there was another knock on the door and she found with joy that it was Hunt.

As he came into the room she asked:

"Does His Lordship want me?"

"No, Ma'am," Hunt replied and Rozella looked at him in surprise at the way he had addressed her.

Then she remembered being told last night that she was "Mrs Lynne" and a relative of Lord Mervyn's.

"What I come to tell you, Ma'am," Hunt went on, "is that your clothes will be arriving later in the morning."

"M-my . . . clothes?" Rozella queried.

"You was in a accident, Ma'am, on the way to Constantinople and though you were rescued, your luggage has all got left behind."

The way Hunt spoke and what he was saying made Rozella begin to laugh. Then she said anxiously:

"If I have to have . . . new clothes . . . I cannot . . .

113

afford anything . . . expensive!''

"There's no need to worry about that, Ma'am," Hunt replied. "His Lordship will see to everything. It's all part of the game, so to speak. Just stay where you are until you've got something decent to put on."

He walked to the door, looked back and gave her what she knew was an impertinent grin and said:

"Every effort's being made, Ma'am, to find your luggage. In the meantime, some clothes'll be arriving which His Lordship hopes'll be to your liking."

As he finished speaking he went out and shut the door while Rozella lay back against her pillows thinking she must be dreaming.

Then as she thought about it, she realised that in a way it was sensible for Lord Mervyn, if he wished to preserve her life, to make quite certain that she, at any rate, was not the woman suspected of being hidden somewhere in the ruined mosque last night.

At the same time, what about himself? Was he taking every precaution?

As she thought about him she realised he was so clever and although he might be unpredictable and at times rude, so obviously useful to the Foreign Office, that it would be a disaster if he were murdered.

When she thought of the men to whom she had listened last night, she knew they were utterly and completely ruthless and that Ayub Khan would stop at nothing to get his own way.

She had hardly had time to consider for herself the monstrous nature of the project he was envisaging, the first move being the murder of the Amir, and then when he was in control of Afghanistan the destruction of the British in India.

"How can he imagine for one moment that his purpose could succeed?" Rozella asked.

She knew that the fanatics of this world had such a faith

114

in themselves and in their Karma that nothing would stop them fighting for what they desired to the very last drop of blood in their bodies.

It was the mad, impossible dream of a man in exile from his country, who must rely on the support of other revolutionaries like himself if he was to succeed.

Rozella lay going over in her mind exactly what he had said, and remembering how Ali Pasha had promised him the support of the Russians.

She realised it was possible for the whole of the East to be set alight by one man's wild ambitions.

'It must not happen!' she thought to herself. 'Please God, it must not happen!'

It was terrifying to think that at the moment only Lord Mervyn and herself held the key to Ayub Khan's secret.

Of course Lord Mervyn was right: it would be a mistake to send a coded message through the British Embassy which might in some way be intercepted.

Rozella realised now that he was planning to leave Turkey with the vital information they had obtained secure in their minds.

Once outside the country it would be easy to put into action the forces that would prevent Ayub Khan from going any further.

If that meant his death, then it was the choice of one man's life against thousands of others.

She had lain thinking it over for about an hour, when there was a knock on the door and a chambermaid ushered in two ladies elegantly dressed and carrying a number of cases.

They set them down on the floor, and a page-boy following behind them brought in several more and a number of bonnet-boxes.

Rozella sat up in bed.

"Good-morning, *Madame!*" one of the women said. "We can only commiserate most deeply at the loss of your luggage, but we have brought some replacements which we hope will please you."

"That is very kind," Rozella murmured.

She could not help feeling excited at the thought of having new clothes, because she had never enjoyed the experience of buying a gown. Everything she wore had been made for her either by her mother or by Nanny.

They could choose only the very cheapest of materials and, although the results had been pretty and becoming, Rozella had been well aware that she was not dressed in the height of fashion.

She had been envious when she had travelled on the Orient Express and had seen how elegantly dressed the other passengers were, especially in the evening when they sat in the Dining-Car, wearing evening-gowns and wraps over them trimmed with sable or marabou.

Now as her visitors began to open the boxes she felt as if she was 'Cinderella' while her Fairy Godmother, in this case in the unlikely guise of Lord Mervyn, was waving a magic wand over her.

She soon learnt from the chatter of the two women who helped her into the garments they brought that they represented the best and most expensive Couturiers in Constantinople.

"Our gowns come from Paris, *Madame*," one of them said, "and our Ladies include the wives of the most important Diplomats and a number of the nobility of Turkey, who in the privacy of their own homes sometimes wear Western attire."

To Rozella's delight they produced gowns so beautiful that she felt she must be dreaming.

There were *toilettes* for the morning and the afternoon and there was a travelling-gown which she was sure was the most suitable for her to wear on the Orient Express.

It brought out the green in her eyes and made her, as one

116

of them said, look like the Spirit of Spring.

Because she had no wish to impose on Lord Mervyn she asked them what his actual orders had been.

"The order was, *Madame*, that you were to have two travelling-gowns to wear on the train, two evening-gowns with wraps to match them in the same material, and anything you fancied for your arrival in Paris."

Rozella drew in her breath.

She could understand Lord Mervyn wishing her to look smart on the train with him, if only to preserve her disguise on their flight from Constantinople.

But she was quite sure that when they reached Paris he would deal with matters without any help from her, and she would be sent back to England.

She therefore chose two travelling-gowns, one with a cape and one with a short jacket to wear over it.

Then she chose two evening-gowns that would not be considered really grand enough to wear at a Ball or an important dinner-party.

However she thought they would compare favourably with those she had seen on the journey out, worn by the very attractive women in the Dining-Car of the train.

Although the two *vendeuses* pressed on her other gowns, she refused but chose the hats which matched her travelling-*ensembles* and thanked them for taking so much trouble.

She had however expressed her thanks too soon, for they had also to provide her with shoes, hand-bags, gloves and some very exquisite underwear.

Never had Rozella imagined anything could be so beautiful as a nightgown and negligée trimmed with lace and little bows of satin ribbon, and underwear appliquéd with lace and tiny stitches onto the purest silk.

Only when the *vendeuses* had left, obviously delighted with the purchases she had made, did she wonder nervously if Lord Mervyn had really meant to spend so much money on her, and might perhaps think she had taken advantage of his generosity.

It was one thing for him to pay for her disguise last night, but quite another to provide what amounted to almost a trousseau of beautiful clothes to wear for the 67 hours, 35 minutes they would be travelling across Europe to Paris.

Then she remembered her mother had said that Lord Mervyn was an extremely rich man, and she supposed decking her out in a fashionable disguise meant no more to him, maybe less, than buying a new hunter.

"At the same time, I shall have to thank him," Rozella thought, and felt shy in case he was disagreeable about it.

When she was dressed in her new gown and looked at herself in the mirror she could hardly believe that she was not actually a stranger who was thinking her thoughts and feeling her feelings.

She was anxious in case Lord Mervyn might not approve of her taste. He might think her gown over-elaborate, and that the hat which went with it trimmed with quills of the same colour as the ribbons encircling it was too theatrical.

Because she had lived so quietly in the country and had never had anything fashionable to wear, she had felt very ignorant and extremely unsophisticated.

It had been bad enough that Lord Mervyn had penetrated her disguise and doubtless thought her ridiculous to have made herself look so hideous for no good reason.

And yet now she was afraid he might think she was over-dressed, flamboyant and, worst of all, unladylike.

She wished frantically that her mother was with her and she could have asked her advice.

Then as she inspected herself once again in the mirror, she knew she had never looked so elegant or indeed, if she was honest, so beautiful.

It would have been difficult for anybody in the village at

home to recognise her, and she was quite certain that no one in the hotel would connect her with the ugly, bespectacled Miss Beverly who had vanished during the night.

She was just wondering what she should do when there was a knock on the door.

She guessed from the sound that it was Hunt, and when he stood there grinning in his usual cheeky manner she felt he was the only friend she had.

"Do . . . I look . . . all right?" she asked.

"You looks smashing, Ma'am!" he answered. "Tip-top as you may say! And there's not a gentleman in the whole of Constantinople as won't say the same!"

Rozella laughed a little shyly and Hunt said:

"His Lordship's wanting to take you out to luncheon."

"Where are we going?"

"To the British Embassy," Hunt replied. "His Lordship's going to introduce you to the Social World, so watch your step! And don't forget you're one of his family."

What Hunt said made Rozella feel more frightened than she was already, but there was no point in saying so. She followed Hunt down the corridor until he opened the Sitting-Room door and said loudly to impress she thought anyone who might be listening:

"Mrs Lynne, M'Lord, and Madam's feeling rested after a good night."

Rozella's heart was beating faster and she found it difficult to walk into the room towards Lord Mervyn who was standing by the window.

She was acutely aware that he was watching her, but he did not move until she was standing just in front of him.

Then as she raised her eyes she saw he was looking at her in what she thought was a strange manner.

Yet with a leap of her heart she realised that for the first time since she had known him there was just a glint of what was undoubtedly admiration in his eyes.

"You had a good night?" he asked.

With an effort Rozella forced herself to understand what he was saying.

"Y-yes . . of course . . thank you . . My Lord."

With her words falling over each other because she was shy she said:

"Thank you . . for the beautiful . . clothes . . I have never possessed . . anything so lovely before."

"They become you," Lord Mervyn said briefly.

There was a silence, then because she could not help herself Rozella asked:

"You are . . pleased with what I was able to tell you . . last night? I . . I did not let you down?"

For a moment Lord Mervyn did not answer and she looked up at him, pleading to be appreciated, her eyes very expressive and at the same time somehow childlike.

Then as if he was choosing his words carefully he said in a deep voice:

"Do I really need to tell you that you were utterly and completely magnificent! No one, not even your father, could have done better!"

Because he spoke with a sincerity she had not expected and in fact had never heard from him before, Rozella felt the colour flooding into her cheeks.

There was a sudden radiance in her eyes as she asked:

"Do you . . mean that? Do you . . really mean it?"

"I mean it!" Lord Mervyn answered. "But it is something we must not talk about here, and in fact must not refer to until we have safely reached Paris."

Because she thought she had been indiscreet, Rozella flushed again. Then she said in a low voice:

"I . . I understand . . and I am happy that you are . . pleased."

"Very pleased."

And there was no doubt that he was speaking the truth.

Chapter Seven

The luncheon at the British Embassy was formal and rather dull.

Rozella managed adroitly to avoid too many questions about her arrival in Constantinople, and Lord Mervyn made things easier by holding the table with a long description of his last visit several years earlier.

When finally they left it was to find Hunt outside with a carriage which also contained their luggage and they drove straight to the station.

Lord Mervyn sat back against the soft cushions and took off his hat.

"That was exhausting," he said, "but you came through it with flying colours!"

Rozella was surprised at the compliment and she looked at him a little shyly before she asked:

"Do you mean that, or are you just . . saying it to please me?"

"I thought you played your part as my relative who had lost her luggage in an accident with an expertise which made me sure you would grace the stage at the Gaiety."

She knew he was teasing her and she laughed before she said:

"I am wondering how many more parts I shall be required to play before I reach home, but it will be sad when the curtain comes down and the drama is ended."

"Personally I think we have had enough drama to last us for a long time," Lord Mervyn remarked curtly.

She was sure then that he had been far more tense and anxious last night than he had revealed at the time.

Perhaps because it was all a new experience to her or, more likely, because she had felt that his being with her was a protection in itself, she had not really been terrified of what might happen.

She had however been really afraid that an unwary slip of their feet, an irrepressible sneeze or cough, might sign their death warrant.

Looking back, she thought she had been confident simply because she was close beside Lord Mervyn that he would win as he always did and would gain the information he wanted which she knew would be vital in the hands of the British.

Whatever Ayub Khan had been planning, it could now be prevented, and she had the feeling, although she did not like to put it into words, that he would not live very long.

All these things flashed through her mind as they drove through the crowded streets towards the station.

The Orient Express, looking very sleek, modern and efficient, was waiting in the station.

Rozella noted that Lord Mervyn was greeted as an old customer, and they were bowed respectfully into their compartments by the Station Master, the attendant of the sleeping-cars and two underlings.

They were side by side with a connecting door between, which Rozella knew would make her feel safe in case she was frightened in the night.

Lord Mervyn tipped everybody generously and Hunt supervised the luggage that was brought in by the porters.

"I'm in a compartment at the end of this coach, M'Lord, in case you needs me," Rozella heard him say to Lord Mervyn.

She went into her own compartment and took off her hat which she knew had an unmistakable Parisian elegance about it, as did her gown.

She looked at herself in the mirror over the seat and

thought how exciting it would be to show her mother her new clothes.

At the same time, if she was honest, she had no wish to leave Lord Mervyn until the last moment, and that, she thought dismally, was something that would happen very soon.

Once they reached Paris and he had conveyed to the Foreign Office what they had discovered, he would no longer have any use for her.

The thought of Paris made her remember that it was a City of beautiful and seductive women.

She remembered how the Princess Eudocia had fawned on him in an endeavour to entice him.

Although that had been for other reasons than that he was an attractive man, Rozella was certain she did not find her appointed task disagreeable.

In Paris there would be women of whom her father had sometimes talked indiscreetly in front of her, thinking she would not understand.

But she knew they were known as the 'demi-mondaines', whose sole purpose in life was to give gentle-men like Lord Mervyn all the joys and pleasures of love.

With a little sigh Rozella turned away from the mirror, thinking how impossible it would be for her to compete with such women, even if she wanted to.

At the same time she wondered why the thought of them left her feeling somehow depressed, as if there was a heavy stone instead of a heart beating in her breast.

The communicating door between her compartment and Lord Mervyn's was ajar and she could hear him talking to Hunt, his voice deep and, she thought, very cultured.

It was the sort of voice a man of his standing should have.

What was so extraordinary was that he was able to change it, as he had when he was dressed as a Turk, to sound very different.

She was sure there were a hundred intonations he could use so cleverly when he was in disguise that no one would suspect that he was not what he professed to be.

She was thinking about him so intently that when he came through the door he seemed to fill the whole compartment.

Almost as if she was looking at him for the first time, she realised how handsome he was, when he was not being supercilious or cynical.

Now he was smiling as he stood beside her, saying as he did so:

"We are just about to leave, and as soon as we are out of Turkey, I feel that we have a great deal to talk about."

He spoke so pleasantly, in fact so charmingly, that Rozella could only smile at him, and she felt there was a sudden light in the compartment which had not been there before.

As Lord Mervyn had been speaking there was the sound of the guard blowing his whistle outside on the platform, and they moved to the window to look out to see those who had been saying goodbye to their friends starting to raise their hands in farewell.

The wheels were turning over, there was a loud hoot from the engine, and a cloud of steam for a moment almost obscured the people on the platform.

Suddenly and so swiftly that she had no time to think, Lord Mervyn turned from the window, threw Rozella down on the floor and flung himself on top of her.

As he did so, there was the sharp crack of a bullet breaking through glass, followed immediately by another which, as the train was moving, broke the glass at the very edge of the window.

Of the two bullets penetrating the carriage, one buried itself in the wood on the far side, the second one in the thick velour covering the seat.

Rozella only knew that she was knocked almost breathless by Lord Mervyn and that her head was on the carpet, while his body, heavy and protective, was crushing her beneath him.

She had heard the sound of both bullets, and only as the train moved quicker and quicker and they were now out of the station did Lord Mervyn raise his head.

He looked down at Rozella and as she looked up at him she was vividly aware of how near he was to her.

Then as they stared without speaking into each other's eyes, Lord Mervyn made a sound that was half an exclamation and half a groan, and his lips came down on Rozella's, holding her captive.

For a moment she could hardly believe it was happening and dazed by the force with which her head had hit the floor she could only feel bewildered.

Then as the pressure of Lord Mervyn's lips increased and his kiss became more possessive and more demanding, she was aware that this was what she had been wanting and longing for, although she had had no idea of it.

At first she was only conscious of the warmth and hardness of his mouth.

Then she felt a strange sensation she had never known rise from her breast into her throat.

She was also vividly aware of the weight and strength of his body and that she was completely helpless beneath him.

As the sensations he was evoking in her intensified and became more acute and at the same time very wonderful, she suddenly knew that she loved him.

What she was feeling was love, exactly as the poets had written about it, only very much more intense.

Lord Mervyn raised his head to look down at her, but Rozella was quite incapable of speech.

She could only stare at him, her eyes seeming to fill her whole face, her lips parted, and her heart beating tumultuously.

For what seemed a long moment he just looked at her.

Then he was kissing her again, kissing her with long, slow, passionate kisses which seemed to draw not only her heart, but her very soul from her body and make it his.

Only when she felt as if no one could know such ecstasy and rapture and not die of the wonder of it, Lord Mervyn said in a voice that seemed strange and very unlike his own:

"My darling, how can you make me feel like this? And yet, I suppose it was inevitable."

It was then that Rozella came back to reality and realised that Lord Mervyn had been on the verge of death and only his quickness had saved him from being murdered.

"T-they . . meant to kill you!" she whispered.

Her voice seemed to come from a long distance and was very frightened.

"They failed!" Lord Mervyn replied. "But it might have been you, my precious, who died."

Then he was kissing her again, kissing her as if he wished to reassure himself that she was alive and only in kisses could he express his feelings.

It seemed a long time later when he said:

"I must be hurting you, my darling."

He moved as he spoke and instinctively Rozella reached out to put her arms around him protectively.

"Be careful . . perhaps you are . . still in . . danger."

He smiled and said:

"I saw my assailant on the platform and, thank God, we have left him behind. At the same time, my lovely one, we have to be very careful until we reach Paris."

"What do you mean . . what are you . . saying?" Rozella asked.

Then without Lord Mervyn explaining she was aware that if his enemies intended to murder him they might have agents waiting on the platforms of the various places where the train would stop on its way to Paris.

Lord Mervyn rose to his feet and pulled Rozella up from the floor where he had thrown her.

He drew her into his arms, and as they sat down together on the seat in which one of the bullets was embedded he was kissing her until she felt it was hard to think or to be aware of anything but her love for him.

Only when it seemed as if he had taken her into a special Heaven where everything was perfect with an indescribable rapture which could not be expressed in words did Lord Mervyn say:

"I must go to find an attendant and have our compartments changed."

Rozella looked at him with frightened eyes and he said:

"I have to take every precaution, my darling, because you are with me. At the same time we are both of us very important because of the secret we carry in our heads, which is vital to the peace of several countries."

Because he spoke so seriously Rozella gave a little cry and put out her hands to hold onto the lapels of his coat.

"You must be careful . . very careful," she said. "If you . . died . . .'

"Would it matter to you if I did?" he interrupted.

She looked up at him, her eyes filled with the love she felt for him, and he knew it was impossible for any woman to look more beautiful.

Her hair was a little untidy from the way he had thrown her to the floor, yet it glinted as if with the fires he felt burning within himself, while her face was flushed with excitement and her lips were quivering a little with the wonder of his kisses.

"I love you!" he said insistently. "God, how much I love you!"

"B-but I thought . . . " Rozella faltered, "I was told in . . England that you . . hated women."

"I not only hated them," Lord Mervyn replied, "but I

believed I was completely immune to their wiles, their attractions, and a maudlin emotion which they called love!"

He saw the consternation in her eyes and added quickly:

"But I want your love, my precious, I want it more than I have ever wanted anything in my whole life! In fact, if I am truthful, nothing matters except that you should love me."

"I *do* love you," Rozella said, "but I had simply no idea of it until I realised with terror that you . . might have been . . shot . . and then you kissed me."

Her voice broke a little and instinctively she moved a little closer to him.

Lord Mervyn's arms tightened and he held her so that it was hard to breathe as he said:

"I was not worrying about myself, but you! If I had been instrumental in causing your death, I think I would have killed myself!"

"How can you . . say such things . . how can you love me . . and so quickly?"

Lord Mervyn smiled before he said:

"I fell in love the moment I saw you."

"That cannot be true!" Rozella exclaimed. "I looked so terrible in my disguise."

"You looked ridiculous, and quite unconvincing."

He gave a short laugh before he added:

"As a disguise it was lamentable!"

She looked away from him a little shyly before she said:

"I was so . . certain I had . . deceived you."

"You did not deceive me for a number of reasons," Lord Mervyn said. "The most important was that as you first came into the room looking, I admit, extremely unattractive, my perception, which your father will tell you is very acute, told me that you were not only different from what you pretended to be, but that you were somebody very special as far as I was concerned."

"I do not believe it!"

"It is true," Lord Mervyn averred. "I did not see the ugliness of the clothes in which you had covered yourself, but what lay beneath them. There was something which vibrated towards me and which, if I am honest, frightened me."

"Frightened you? How could it?" Rozella enquired.

"You awoke in me all the feelings I thought I had crushed and set aside from myself for ever. Then, my darling, when you spoke to me, I fell in love with your voice."

"My . . voice?" Rozella questioned.

"Have you any idea how soft and musical, and very, very feminine it is?"

She gave a little laugh and put her cheek against his as he went on:

"I had never listened to any sound so attractive, and I knew then, even before I reasoned it out logically for myself, that you were not the middle-aged woman you pretended to be! Then, after I had fallen in love with your voice, I found your lips completely irresistible."

As he spoke he put his fingers under her chin and turned her face up to his.

"And that is what I am finding them now," he said and kissed her again.

It was a long kiss which left Rozella speechless, while her heart beat frantically with a wild excitement which she sensed Lord Mervyn was feeling too.

"I cannot believe you are . . saying these . . things to me," she whispered. "I . . I think I must be . . dreaming."

"If you are, then I am dreaming too."

He kissed her again, then deliberately setting her a little aside from him he said:

"I have to go and see the attendant. Take care of yourself, my precious! I am half afraid that when I come back I shall find you have vanished and were only a mirage."

"I shall be here," Rozella replied. "But are you quite sure it is . . safe for you to go . . out of the . . compartment?"

"It is a risk I have to take," Lord Mervyn answered, "for the simple reason that I have no intention of being here when we reach the next station."

He went without saying any more and Rozella put her hands up to her face feeling that his declaration of love could not be true, and must be a figment of her imagination.

How could he love her when he was a misogynist? How could she love him when she had been so certain when she first met him that she hated him?

She felt her whole body pulsating with her love, and it seemed to her that she waited a century of time before he came back.

He had the attendant with him in the corridor and there was also Hunt.

"It is all right," Lord Mervyn said quietly to Rozella, "there are two empty compartments in the next coach and we are moving into them."

Rozella picked up her hat and Lord Mervyn helped her as she walked a little unsteadily down the corridor of the swiftly travelling train into the next coach.

The two compartments there were identical to the ones they had left, and she reasoned without asking questions that if Lord Mervyn's assailants had telegraphed to anybody down the line to make another attempt on his life, they would have described the exact position of his compartment on the train which would be easier than describing what he looked like.

When the luggage had been changed and they were alone together again Lord Mervyn said:

"Do not look so worried, my precious! There is every chance that we are now quite safe, and it is in fact, very unlikely that either Ayub Khan or Ali Pasha will have

130

followers or agents on any of the stations at which we stop before we reach Paris."

He kissed her hand before he added:

"At the same time, I am taking no chances where you are concerned."

"It is . . you they want to . . kill!" Rozella said in a frightened voice.

"They will remember that I was not alone," Lord Mervyn said, "and it really would be wise, my precious, for us to separate until we reach our journey's end."

Rozella gave a little cry.

"No . . no . . I could not . . bear it! I cannot . . leave you!"

Lord Mervyn looked at her before he said:

"That is what I hoped you would say, and I feel the same! Indeed there is no reason why they should connect a very beautiful and elegantly dressed 'Mrs Lynne' with the ageing, somewhat grotesque figure of Miss Beverly."

Because of the laughter in his voice Rozella blushed and hid her face against his shoulder.

"I feel . . embarrassed now," she said, "when I remember you . . saw me looking . . so awful."

"I have already told you," Lord Mervyn said, "that I did not look at you with my eyes, but with my heart."

Rozella drew in her breath.

"Promise me that you will always look at me like that and . . love me."

"That is a very easy thing to do," Lord Mervyn said, "for I love you as I never thought I would love anybody. In fact, I would have staked my entire fortune against it!"

"But you were wrong . . you really were wrong!"

He drew her closer to him as he said:

"I love you so overwhelmingly, so completely, that I wonder now how I could have been such an idiot as to believe I could live without love and that it was of no importance in my life."

He laughed again as he said:

"I suppose like a great many men I was over-confident and far too sure of myself! Now I know there is no defence against a rapture which can only come from Heaven."

"That is what you have given me," Rozella said, "but I . . feel I have to . . look after you and . . protect you."

"Just as I intend to protect you, my precious," Lord Mervyn replied.

Rozella moved a little closer to him as she said:

"Promise me that you will take no risks with yourself in the future. I thought it was very exciting and a great adventure when I took Papa's place, but now that I know how dangerous it was and how very nearly you could have died, I do not want to have to think about it again."

"We will have enough other things to do in the future my darling, without undertaking any more secret missions on behalf of the Foreign Office."

"Do you really mean that?"

"I mean that it is time I settled down on my estate in England," Lord Mervyn replied, "and had a family as well as a wife to care for."

He waited to see the colour come into Rozella's cheeks and laughed softly.

"We have so many things to do together, so much excitement, so many inexpressible delights, that there will be no need for our lives to become involved in disguises and espionage."

"That is what I wanted you to tell me."

"I would much rather talk about us," Lord Mervyn replied. "How soon can we be married, my lovely one?"

There was a little silence before Rozella said in a small voice:

"Are you . . quite sure you . . want to marry me? After all, if you do, you may find that . . once again you are . . hating women."

"I have every intention of marrying you," Lord Mervyn

said firmly. "The only question you have to answer is whether you will marry me in Paris or make me wait until we get home."

"Marry you in Paris?" Rozella exclaimed in surprise. "But . . how can we do that?"

"Very easily," Lord Mervyn replied. "The moment we arrive we are going to the British Embassy. We will stay there where we shall be completely safe, just in case there is any trouble, although I think now that is very unlikely and the British Embassy Church is close by."

"And . . we can be married . . there?"

"Why not?" he asked. "Quite frankly, I do not want to lose you, not even into another bedroom at night. I want you with me, I want you beside me, I want to be quite certain that you are mine, and nothing and nobody can part us."

He spoke with a passion in his voice which Rozella had not heard before, and as she looked up at him wide-eyed feeling it almost impossible to assimilate everything that was happening, he said:

"I am in love, my sweet, so wildly, ecstatically, over-whelmingly in love, that all I want is to make you mine and to know that neither God nor man can ever separate us again."

Because she found the way he spoke irresistible Rozella said:

"That is . . what I want . . too."

Lord Mervyn looked at her as if he was afraid she was not real.

Then he was kissing her, kissing her demandingly, as if he would make her his from that moment to Eternity.

When they reached Paris they went straight to the British Embassy.

The Ambassador was the Marquess of Dufferin, who was, as soon as they were alone with him, extremely interested in what Lord Mervyn had to tell him.

He himself had been at the Embassy in Constantinople before he went to India as Viceroy, and he realised perhaps better than anyone else the danger presented by Ayub Khan.

"Thank God you got away safely!" he exclaimed.

"Only by the skin of our teeth," Lord Mervyn answered, and told the Ambassador how they had been fired on when they were leaving the station.

The Marquess then helped them to prepare the coded report of what they had learnt and promised to send a Courier with it immediately to Lord Granville at the Foreign Office.

While he was talking Rozella thought Lord Mervyn was even more impressive than he had been described to her by her father.

In fact, she thought the two men talking together, though the Marquis was much older, might have been two gods sitting on Olympus, directing the lives of human beings.

When their business was finished and once again the Ambassador had congratulated them on what he said was a brilliant coup, Lord Mervyn said:

"And now, My Lord, I would like to talk about something more personal. Miss Beverly has promised to marry me, and we would like our wedding to take place immediately, partly for security reasons, and partly because I have no wish to return to England until she is my wife."

"This is a great surprise!" the Marquis exclaimed.

The way he spoke told Rozella that he, like everybody else, had thought Lord Mervyn was a misogynist.

"However," he went on, "we will certainly see that your wedding is a memorable one."

"I want it to be as quiet as possible," Lord Mervyn said sharply.

"That is what I would have expected of you," the Am-

134

bassador smiled, "but I am sure my wife will have different ideas!"

This made Rozella rather anxious, but when she met the Marchioness she had no fears that Lord Mervyn's wish for a quiet wedding would be challenged.

The Marchioness of Dufferin was a very sweet, rather shy woman who adored her volcanic husband and had spent her marriage trying to protect him in every way she could, but unobtrusively and remaining very much 'in the shadow of the throne'.

She was however delighted that Lord Mervyn was to be married.

"I am so glad, dear," she said gently to Rozella, "that you have cured him of this ridiculous idea that he does not like women. My husband has always admired him for his brilliance in the missions he has undertaken, and it was only when he stayed here with us and ignored the most beautiful, charming and delightful women, however beguiling they were, that we realised something was missing in his life. Now I know it was you!"

The way she spoke made Rozella nervous, and when she was alone with Lord Mervyn she said to him:

"Our hostess has . . frightened . . me."

"How did she do that?"

"She was so surprised," Rozella explained, "that you should be . . interested in me, after you have refused to . . notice very much more . . alluring ladies."

She hesitated for a moment before she went on:

"Suppose . . when we are married you . . decide after all that you . . hate women and . . wish you were . .single again?"

The way she spoke told Lord Mervyn it was a very real fear, and he put his arms around her and drew her close to him before he said:

"Listen my darling, I want you to understand once and

135

for all that what I feel for you is different from anything I have ever felt for anyone! Because I know that what you have given me is real love, it will not fade or wither, but be with us all our lives."

The way he spoke was so moving that Rozella felt the tears come into her eyes.

"You are . . sure . . really sure?" she whispered.

"Absolutely sure!"

He kissed her in a way that told her there would be no more arguments about it.

The Marchioness of Dufferin was determined that however quietly they were to be married in the British Embassy Church, Rozella should look like a bride.

"It is your first wedding, my dear," she said, "and I am sure your last, and it is something you will want always to remember."

Although Lord Mervyn and the Ambassador were making arrangements for the wedding to take place the following day, the Marchioness managed to obtain from her own dressmaker in Paris a wedding-gown which made Rozella gasp when she saw it.

She also provided her with the lace veil she had worn at her own wedding and a magnificent diamond tiara.

When she was dressed Rozella knew that the Marchioness had been right: not only would she remember this moment when she became Lord Mervyn's wife as the most exciting and beautiful in her life, but also she was sure he would remember it too.

"You remind me of my own wedding," the Marchioness said softly as she put the finishing touches to Rozella's glittering tiara, then pulled the veil over her face.

"I am just . . hoping that I shall . . make him happy," Rozella said.

"If you are as happy as we have been," the Marchioness replied, "no one could ask for more."

136

They went from the bedroom and as they descended the stairs and Rozella saw the Ambassador waiting for her in the hall, she realised that from this moment her whole life had altered, and she was stepping into the unknown.

Just for a moment she was afraid, then she knew that if she were with Lord Mervyn she would never be afraid again either physically or mentally.

When she saw him waiting for her at the steps of the altar in the little Church and the Ambassador took her up the aisle, she wanted to run to his side and slip her hand into his.

Instead they processed slowly, and as the Marchioness who had gone ahead of them took her seat in the first pew, there was nobody else in the Church except for the parson who was to marry them.

And yet Rozella felt as if they were compassed about with a great cloud of witnesses, and she was sure that the voices she heard in her heart were Angels singing with happiness.

Lying in bed in the Bridal Suite at the Hotel Rozella moved a little closer to her husband.

"Are you awake, my darling one?" he asked.

"I thought you were asleep," she answered.

"I am too happy to sleep," he replied. "I was just lying, thinking about you, and feeling that I am the most fortunate man in the world."

"I was telling myself I am the most fortunate of women," Rozella said. "How could I have imagined when I left England knowing that your money would save Papa's life, that Lord Mervyn, the misogynist, would become my husband?"

Lord Mervyn laughed and it was a very happy sound.

"It sounds strange when you put it like that, but I had simply never doubted that your father would want to join

137

me in what I knew would be a very unusual adventure in which his enormous knowledge of languages was essential."

He pulled Rozella against him before he said:

"The first thing we will do when we get back to England, my darling, is to see that your father has the finest Physicians available. I think it would be a good idea if, while we go to the country, your father and mother stayed at my house in London so that there will be no difficulties about his having the very best treatment which the doctors can prescribe.'

"That would be very kind of you," Rozella said, "but the most important thing is that the money you sent Papa has been providing the food necessary to build up his strength."

Lord Mervyn's arms tightened.

"I cannot bear to think of any of you being so poor and actually hungry!" he said. "But all that is finished now, and I blame myself deeply that I did not look after your father better in the past, knowing how brilliant he was."

"You really think . . that?" Rozella asked.

"Of course I think it, and I intend to see that he is given the recognition he deserves in the future."

He knew as he finished speaking that Rozella was asking wordlessly what that would be and he said:

"He might be happiest as the head of the Oriental Languages Department in the University of London, or perhaps Oxford, but one thing I promise you, my precious, I will see that his salary is one which will enable your mother to have everything she wants in life, just as I intend to give her daughter everything and anything she needs."

"All I really want," Rozella said, "is your love . . but I also love you for thinking of my parents, and giving Papa what he deserves."

"I will do that, and a great deal more," Lord Mervyn promised, "not only because I admire your father, but also

138

because I do not want you to worry about him."

He kissed her forehead before he added:

"I am selfish enough to want you to worry only about me."

"I shall always do that," Rozella said. "How could I help it, when you have been so brave and in serving England have made a number of enemies of whom I shall always be afraid?"

"You are not to think about them again!" Lord Mervyn commanded. "They all belong in my past, just as you are not to remember that I was once a misogynist."

"When I think it over," Rozella replied, "I want you to continue to be a misogynist as far as every other woman is concerned!"

"Are you telling me that you are jealous?"

"Of course I am jealous! Do not forget, I had to save you from Princess Eudocia, and I only hope I do not have to do the same thing in the case of a great number of other attractive and beautiful women!"

"If there are other attractive and beautiful women, as you call them, in the world, I shall not be aware of them," Lord Mervyn said. "You fill my whole being, Rozella, my eyes, my heart, and, if I have one, my soul."

"That is what I want you to say," she answered, "and yet, I am very proud of my handsome, attractive husband, and I realise that at the Reception which the Ambassador gave for us after our wedding there was not a woman in the Embassy who would not have been only too delighted to change places with me!"

Lord Mervyn laughed.

"Now you are flattering me! And if we are being truthful, you must have been aware that every man present was looking at you with admiration in his eyes and thinking what a very lucky man I am!"

He did not wait for Rozella to reply, but turned towards her saying in a different tone of voice:

"And that is what I am – lucky because you are everything a man could want in a wife. You are not only beautiful, but so adorable that every moment I am with you I find something about you which makes me love you more."

Rozella gave a little cry and put her arm around his neck.

"I love you . . I love you!" she said. "And every time you kiss me . . and when you touch me . . I find my love increases until it fills the whole world and the sky."

She drew in her breath and added:

"And when you . . make love to me . . you lift me up to the stars . . and I feel as if they are still flickering inside me . . and yet they are . . burning like the sun."

"And that is how I feel too," Lord Mervyn said.

Then as his lips found Rozella's she knew that the fire within her breast was only part of the fire that burned in him.

As the flames grew higher and higher, their love carried them into the sky.

And they knew an ecstasy and a rapture which is part of the Eternal love from which no one can ever escape.

Other books by Barbara Cartland

Romantic Novels, over 400, the most recently published being:
The Love Trap
Listen to Love
The Golden Cage
Love Casts out Fear
A World of Love
Dancing on a Rainbow
Love Joins the Clan
An Angel Runs Away
Forced to Marry
Bewildered in Berlin
A Wedding Ring
Starlight
The Earl Escapes
True Love
Love and Kisses
Sapphires in Siam
A Caretaker of Love
Secrets of the Heart
Riding to the Sky
Lovers in Lisbon

The Dream and the Glory (in aid of the St John Ambulance Brigade)

Autobiographical and biographical:
The Isthmus Years 1919–1939
The Years of Opportunity 1939–1945
I Search for Rainbows 1945–1975
We Danced All Night 1919–1929
Ronald Cartland (With a Foreword by Sir Winston Churchill)
Polly – My Wonderful Mother
I Seek the Miraculous

Historical:
Bewitching Women
The Outrageous Queen (the Story of Queen Christina of
Sweden)
The Scandalous Life of King Carol
The Private Life of Charles II
The Private Life of Elizabeth, Empress of Austria
Josephine, Empress of France
Diane de Poitiers
Metternich – the Passionate Diplomat

Sociology:
You in the Home
The Fascinating Forties
Marriage for Moderns
Be Vivid, Be Vital
Love, Life and Sex
Vitamins for Vitality
Husbands and Wives
Men are Wonderful
Etiquette for Love and Romance
Etiquette
Barbara Cartland's Book of Health
The Many Facets of Love
Sex and the Teenager
The Book of Charm
Living Together
The Youth Secret
The Magic of Honey
The Book of Beauty and Health

Keep Young and Beautiful by Barbara Cartland and Elinor
Glyn

Cookery:
Barbara Cartland's Health Food and Cookery Book
Food for Love
Magic of Honey Cookbook
Recipes for Lovers
The Romance of Food

Editor of:
The Common Problem by Ronald Cartland (with a preface by the Rt. Hon. the Earl of Selborne, P.C.)
Barbara Cartland's Library of Love
Barbara Cartland's Library of Ancient Wisdom

Written with Love
Passionate love letters selected by Barbara Cartland

Drama:
Blood Money
French Dressing

Philosophy:
Touch the Stars

Radio Operetta:
The Rose and the Violet (Music by Mark Lubbock) performed in 1942.

Radio Plays:
The Caged Bird: An episode in the Life of Elizabeth Empress of Austria. Performed in 1957.

General:
Barbara Cartland's Book of Useless Information, with a Foreword by The Earl Mountbatten of Burma. (In aid of the United World Colleges)
Love and Lovers Picture Book

The Light of Love (Prayer Book)
Barbara Cartland's Scrapbook (in Aid of the Royal Photographic Museum)
Romantic Royal Marriages
Barbara Cartland's Book of Celebrities
Getting Older. Growing Younger

Verse:
Lines on Life and Love

Music:
An Album of Love Songs sung with the Royal Philharmonic Orchestra.

Film
The Flame is Love

Cartoons:

Children's Book:
The Princess to the Rescue

Barbara Cartland Romances: (Book of Cartoons) has recently been published in the U.S.A. and Great Britain and in other parts of the world.